When they came to another log Rowan turned
Swallow to face it and pressed him into a trot. What
possessed her to do this she had no idea, only the
memory of seeing him flying over the timber in the
wood with Hugh leaning up on his neck and
remembering her feeling of longing that it might be
herself . . . and Swallow lengthened his stride and flew
the log, so effortlessly that she did not budge in the
saddle. True, it was only small, but Rowan felt as if she
were riding for England at Badminton. Her
confidence swelled and took off like a hot air balloon,
so that it was all she could do to stop belting off
down the inviting path for the sheer hell of it.

'What on earth do you two think you're doing?'

An angry voice interrupted her moment of glory and
she looked up to see Charlie coming down the track
ahead of her, riding Out of the West. Swallow skidded
to a halt and Hugh ambled up on Honeypot. To
Rowan's dismay Charlie was obviously furious, and
his dark blue gaze was directed straight at her.

She had no excuse at all . . .

Also available by K. M. Peyton,
and published by Corgi Books:

The High Horse series:
THE SWALLOW TALE

For younger readers:
POOR BADGER

K. M. PEYTON

THE
SWALLOW
SUMMER

Illustrated by the author

CORGI BOOKS

THE SWALLOW SUMMER
A CORGI BOOK : 0 552 52969 9

First published in Great Britain by Doubleday,
a division of Transworld Publishers Ltd

PRINTING HISTORY
Doubleday edition published 1995
Corgi edition published 1997

Corgi Books are published by Transworld Publishers Ltd,
61–63 Uxbridge Road, London W5 5SA,
in Australia by Transworld Publishers (Australia) Pty Ltd,
15–25 Helles Avenue, Moorebank, NSW 2170,
and in New Zealand by Transworld Publishers (NZ) Ltd,
3 William Pickering Drive, Albany, Auckland.

Printed and bound in Great Britain by
Cox & Wyman Ltd, Reading, Berkshire.

To Alison

CHAPTER ONE

'Am I going to Pony Club camp?' Rowan asked Charlie Hawes. She didn't have a pony to take, and Charlie had several.

'Of course,' he said. And smiled, as she turned noticeably first red, then white.

'It's fun,' he said gently. 'Not terrible.'

'I can't ride!'

'Lots of them can't ride. You won't be alone. And think, by the end of the week, how much you will have improved!'

'Who on?' Her voice was a whisper. She wanted, longed, above all else, that it would be Swallow.

Charlie knew her thoughts, and shook his head.

'No, not Swallow.'

Rowan tried not to let her bitter disappointment show. If she was honest, the disappointment was tinged slightly with relief. Swallow always bucked her off: he had been labelled a rogue and only the

Hawes could ride him. There were five of them and they all rode like those born to it – on a horse before they could walk. Instinctive. Even Lizzie, the middle one, who was thirteen and the most nervous, who said she only rode because she had to, was an elegant and sympathetic rider. Hugh, eleven like Rowan, was (unlike Rowan) brave, brilliant and boastful. Rowan, having moved into the village only recently and discovered the magic of the horse world, knew she would never, never, never – however much she improved – be able to ride like a Hawes. But she longed to ride 'her' pony, Swallow.

Charlie disappeared into the feed shed and Rowan went round to see Swallow in his loose-box. In the stable he was the kindest pony in the world: friendly and affectionate, his bold eyes gleaming with curiosity from beneath the black wing of his forelock. He, and several others, had been bought by Charlie from a run-down riding school, in very bad condition, but a few weeks on good grass and feed had worked wonders, and Swallow was almost back to his bright self, a handsome, fourteen-hand Welshman, dark brown in colour, with a blueish sheen over his quarters that had prompted Rowan to christen him Swallow. Strange how she was drawn to this pony . . . Rowan was the first to admit the silliness of it, when he was so unsuitable. But ever since she had first set eyes on him she had adored him, and no other pony would measure up. Instead of saying she was stupid, Charlie said it worked that way sometimes. He had been drawn to the raw-boned, thin bay called Wilfred that had stood forlorn in the back of the awful riding stable. He had bought him and been laughed to scorn by the rest of the family. Rowan adored seventeen-year-old Charlie because, instead of being brisk with her dreams, he was sympathetic.

'We all have dreams,' he said. 'And sometimes they happen. Fairy tales. After all, somebody has to win gold.'

Win gold! Perhaps a mauve rosette at the Pony Club . . . that would be gold to Rowan. As she ran her hand down Swallow's warm, shining neck, she had no illusions about what lay ahead.

*　　*　　*

Charlie went into the house, which slept like a tawny lion amongst the tangle of his mother's generously planted garden on the uphill side of the stable yards. Of golden sandstone and thatch, it had looked out over the valley of Long Bottom for five hundred years and, in truth, not a great deal had changed in that time. Rowan, fresh from London with her smart parents, thought it was paradise, but sometimes Charlie wondered what he was missing. He had always assumed he would go off somewhere when the opportunity arose and find his place in the world, but since his father's death, his future had closed down. He was committed, along with his older sister Josephine, to keeping the family together at High Hawes and making a living out of the place, as his father had done. It had been a democratic vote, and he had been the first to agree to it, but sometimes . . . well, he couldn't say teaching the Blue Ride at Pony Club camp was the most exciting thing in a chap's immediate future – slightly embarrassing, if the truth were known, mixing with the green wellie brigade, the admirable middle-aged ladies with whiskers on their chins and Labradors at their heels who steered the little girls across country with cries of 'Legs! Legs! *Ride*, Fiona!'

His father had been a hard-bitten horse dealer and a tough master to work for. Having him off his back was in many ways a relief for Charlie, but the responsibility of having to make money out of what he had formerly thought of as mostly pleasure was daunting. It was his mother Joan who had – before her husband died – pointed out that the area was rife with little girls who wanted riding lessons and had nowhere to go, and that High Hawes could easily fill this need. This now seemed the best course to take and the children had decided the farm would be called High Horse Stables. This was Hugh's idea. 'Very clever, don't you think?' Moderately, Charlie thought. Joan said, 'I know you think you've outgrown the Pony Club, Charlie, but it would be very valuable to the stable if you get back in there and show them that we have a private school at hand, nice ponies, and knowledgeable, friendly people to help them. Only a small proportion of them these days know one end of a pony from the other. They're all down from London like Rowan's people and they get in terrible tangles. Millie Mildmay would love you to teach at camp – you and Josephine – she told me so. And it would get the stable known and do us all a lot of good.'

Joan Hawes always talked sense. Charlie knew it. But his heart did not rise up singing at the thought of reporting to Millie Mildmay.

'The more you mix with local people, the better it will be for the business. A summer with the Pony Club will open up all sorts of contacts. Did you know, for example, that old Millie has bludgeoned Jerry Patterson into joining the committee? I'm not sure that he knows it yet but she's after using his stable yard for Pony Club camp. He's a man after your own heart, I would have thought. Why don't you ride over and have a chat with him?'

Jerry Patterson was a racehorse trainer in the next valley. He was young, struggling and notoriously unsuccessful, but his enthusiasm kept his yard in business. His horses were hurdlers and chasers that raced in the winter, not on the flat, so his yard was largely empty in the summer. Millie Mildmay was his aunt and, such was her clout, nearly everybody did what she told them.

Charlie decided to take his mother's advice. He didn't see what good it would do him, but any excuse to visit a racing stable was all right by him, and he liked Jerry. It was a glorious day, sunny with a fresh breeze, and the more slow riding Wilfred got to build up his muscles, the better. He went back across the garden and through the gate into the back stable yard. They kept their own horses here; the front one, with an archway on to the lane, was the smart yard, his father's old dealing yard, but it was empty now. They had sold all his horses since he had died, and the riding school ponies which would replace them were out at grass, filling out their ribs. Teaching little girls was a start, and it was true that the market was there, but Charlie dreamed of a competition yard full of event horses (which he would ride). He liked thoroughbreds, and bloodlines that went back to Hyperion and St Simon and Eclipse. Wilfred was a thoroughbred, although he didn't look much like one at present. Charlie, because he had an instinct for such things, could see a well-made, straight-actioned young horse underneath the sad, thin-necked, dull-eyed animal he went to saddle up.

'Poor old fellow! You drew a short straw, getting into that dud stable. Trust me, Wilfred, your luck has changed.'

The horse turned his head and gave Charlie a resigned look. He had large eyes, which should have been bold and keen, long ears, and a kind, handsome head. He was a bay with black points, and no white save for a narrow stripe down his face. He stood just over sixteen hands. Charlie would have liked two inches more, for he was tall and still growing. But Charisma, a world champion, had been no more than fifteen two.

'It's heart that matters, Wilfred. And who knows how big yours is? We'll have to find out.'

He led him out and Rowan, watching, saw a

very plain and boring horse, and wondered why on earth Charlie had bought him for himself. Because he was cheap, she supposed.

'Why don't you come with me? I'm hacking over to Sand House. Slowly. Find yourself a pony.'

Rowan's face lit up like the sun bursting out of cloud. She was alone because all the younger Hawes had gone, en masse, to the dentist. Josephine, the eldest, was giving a lesson in the manège. They could hear her voice: 'Use your inside leg! Feel the rein, don't yank!' A child's voice answered plaintively, 'Nothing happens!' Josephine was trying to keep her cool. Teaching, even when you knew it all yourself, was not as easy as she had supposed.

'Who on?' Rowan asked.

The 'easy' pony she generally rode, Fable, was in the lesson, as was the other easy one, a chestnut cob known as the Armchair. Hugh wouldn't want her riding his pony Cascade, and Snowball, the other possibility, was as far away down the big field as it was possible to be. Swallow put his head over his door and whinnied. Charlie hesitated.

Then he said, 'I'm only walking, all the way. How about Swallow?'

Even as he spoke, a voice inside him cried

out, 'Fool! Idiot!' But Rowan, already ecstatic at the thought of riding out with him, now looked about to burst with joy.

'Swallow! Really, do you mean it?'

How could he say, No, I've changed my mind?

'Yes,' he said. 'Why not?'

Why not, after all? If the beast started to play up, he could put her on the leading rein. He sensibly fetched a lead-rope, in case, and tied it round his waist where he hoped Rowan wouldn't notice it. She tacked up, fetched her hat, and led Swallow out. Charlie held him while she mounted, and adjusted the stirrups for her, then vaulted on to Wilfred. Already Rowan's eager face was flushed with apprehension. Her knuckles showed white as she clutched the reins.

'Relax,' Charlie said. 'Let his mouth alone. Ask him nothing. He'll follow Wilfred without your doing anything. Plenty of rein.'

To her surprise, Swallow went like a lamb behind Wilfred out into the lane. Charlie headed up the hill towards the downs above the farmhouse. There was an oak wood that circled the uphill side of the house, and the Hawes had made a ride through it that opened out on to the downs without going on the road. The path was peaty and soft and the sunlight came through the trees in golden swathes. A green woodpecker flew ahead of them like a tropical parrot, shrieking. When they came through into the open again on to a chalky path that climbed up steadily to the top of the down, Rowan felt her whole body bound with a sense of freedom and bliss, to be where she was, with Charlie alone, on her beloved Swallow . . . it had never happened before. She had ridden up here, but only on Fable or Diamond, with Hugh showing off on Cascade, and Lizzie and Shrimp quarrelling – happily, but never like this: ecstatically. White clouds soared across the horizon against a brilliant blue sky, and the warm smell of the downland turf tickled their nostrils. Rowan had never ridden over the top, where they were going now. She would follow Charlie to the world's end.

'Nice, isn't it?' he said.

Rowan could not trust herself to speak.

Swallow felt keen beneath her, but it was uphill all the way and she felt in control. She tried not to hold his mouth, and told herself to relax. Josephine had told her she was too tense, and that conveyed nervousness to the horse. 'They really do know what you are thinking, you know.' Wilfred, with his long, easy stride, walked slightly ahead, and Rowan could see how easily Charlie sat in the saddle. He was slender and wiry, his body hard as nails, and rode with an unstudied elegance. He was the dark one of the family, with thick, black hair and dark, sapphire-blue eyes – 'a gypsy like his father' they said in the village – and he had a magic, gypsy way with a horse. Unlike the other Hawes children, he had skipped a lot of school to work with his father and make money by mending and trading in old cars and agricultural machinery. The other four Hawes were studious and intelligent, but Charlie was clever in a different sort of way. And unlike the others he understood Rowan's misgivings and fear, and the strange compulsion that made her want to ride Swallow instead of sweet Fable and the harmless Armchair.

Charlie turned off the chalk track to take a short cut over the top of the down. The grass was steep and Rowan could feel Swallow's powerful quarters working beneath her. His glossy summer coat rippled over his shoulders and the wind blew back his heavy mane. Coming over the brow, the view into the next valley opened up like a map, dappled with moving clouds, the villages and roads below etched out in the sunshine like a child's toy set. Behind them, turning in the saddle, Rowan could look down and see High Hawes nestling behind its oak wood and the village of Long Bottom sprawled below it. The white dot was Snowball in the bottom field, and the piebald specks on the far side of the valley were Mr Bailey's Friesian cows with, no doubt, Barbara Bailey's knock-kneed pony, Black Diamond, amongst them. She could even see her own house in the village, and Matty Prebble's show-jumps like coloured matchsticks in their field.

Swallow wheeled beneath her as Wilfred set off again, anxious to keep close. But Rowan relaxed (it was hard) and nothing untoward happened. The wind raced up towards them, flattening the grass into patterns and blowing out the horses' tails, and Charlie turned to see if she was all right, and smiled.

The village below was a haunt of racehorses, with several stable yards opening off the through road. Gallops were marked out on the far down, sheltered by long strips of woodland, and a couple of strings could be seen working. Jerry Patterson's yard stood on its own, two miles out of the village up a long chalky drive. It was in a bowl of downland, hidden from sight, and one came upon it with surprise and – in Rowan's case – delight. Unlike most of the yards which were purpose-built and severe-looking, this place dated back to the last century and the stable yard was built round a grassy sort of green with an enormous walnut tree growing in the middle. The stables were beautiful but, undeniably, falling apart. Some of the tiled roofs had fallen in and the rows of dormers over the sagging stable doors were at odd angles as the supporting beams had given way. Outside the yard, with its back to the rising ground behind it, was a very dilapidated Victorian house.

They rode into the deserted stable yard and pulled up. Two pigeons flew up out of the walnut tree and rattled away, then it was quite silent, save for the distant trilling of skylarks on the down.

'What do you think of it?' Charlie asked.

'I think it's a wonderful place. So lonely.'

'Derby winners lived in these boxes once. It was a very famous yard a hundred years ago. Look, I'll show you.'

He slipped down from Wilfred and led him across to an open loose-box. Its door creaked in the breeze, scraping on the ground. Looking in, Rowan saw a huge box lined all round with mahogany and, above that, with white tiles. The manger was of porcelain, and there were brass tie-rings above it. The floor was tiled, with grooves leading to a drain in the middle.

'They don't make stables like this any more,' Charlie said.

They led Wilfred and Swallow in and tied them side by side, one with Charlie's lead-rope and the other with a bit of binder twine Charlie found, to the noseband. They loosened the girths and ran up the stirrups and shut the door on the two of them.

Jerry was in the house, making a phone call, and gestured to them to go through into the kitchen where two lurchers dozed in a patch of sunlight by the open door. The kettle was still warm and Charlie helped himself to coffee, and one for Rowan. The kitchen was in chaos, but comfortably so, rather than squalidly. Jerry came in shortly and greeted them. Rowan was introduced.

'I hear you're going into business – High Horse, isn't it called? And Aunt Millie tells me you're going to teach at camp – she ropes in everybody, the old bag, for her wretched Pony Club. Me too. She wants to bring the lot here! She thinks it's ideal – three miles from the nearest pub. I remember getting out at night and going to the pub was the best bit of Pony Club camp. And smuggling it back in.'

'Yeah.' Charlie grinned. His memories were more recent than Jerry's, but similar. He wasn't sure how he was going to fare, being on the side of authority.

Jerry was older than Charlie but not by all that much, considering the responsibilities of his job. He was a large man – too heavy to ride racehorses, his life's catastrophe. Training them was the next best thing. He had a natural, bounding optimism which showed in his cheerful face and laughter.

'Thank God you'll be one of the party. I'll want some male support. She's taking the house over, you know, catering in the kitchen – I'll have to clear it all up a bit before the day. I'm going to move out, even if it means sleeping over at the stables.'

'You could come home with me. Ma'll put you up.'

'Dogs as well?'

'Sure. The house'll be empty, with the kids over here.'

'That's great! What a relief! Glad you called.'

They went back to the stable yard and the two lurchers got up and padded silently behind Jerry. Jerry inspected Wilfred and appeared to see what Rowan failed to: 'Very nice when you get him fit. Great front. Nice pony too.'

Charlie beamed. 'Yeah, we need more like

him – size and type, I mean, not temperament. He's a bit of a devil.'

'There's one down the road going begging. Belongs to a girl who doesn't like riding. Her mother asked me if I could find it some work. Not much bothered about selling – they've tons of money, but no grass. It's bored rigid in a straw yard at the moment. Want to go and see it?'

'Yes! Great.'

So Jerry got in his old banger, followed by the two dogs. Charlie and Rowan got their mounts out of the loose-box and followed him at a steady trot down the drive and towards the village. He turned into the first farmyard they came to. As they rode in behind him a whinny came from one of the barns and Rowan saw an eager movement, as the pony came to see what visitors had arrived.

The pony was much like Swallow in size and shape but had a less thrusting presence. It was a dark blue-roan with a pretty head, sensible looking.

'It's called Jones,' Jerry said. 'It's quite nice, as far as I know, no vices. Shall I raise its owner? I know she's dying to get rid of him.'

'Could be one for you, Rowan,' Charlie said. He saw her expression and laughed. 'Until Swallow's settled down.'

He realized that Rowan thought one ride over the downs following Wilfred, during which she hadn't fallen off, meant that time had already arrived.

Jerry went and fetched a rather smart lady from a house a little further on, and she agreed happily that Charlie should take the pony there and then. She looked at Wilfred's thin flanks rather dubiously, but they explained that he was newly bought out of a bad home and that Jones would be more than happy where he was going. She never said anything about money.

'Wonders never cease,' Charlie remarked, after they had said farewell to Jerry and his dogs and set off back the way they had come with Jones on the lead rein. 'That visit certainly paid off.'

Rowan tucked in behind, sure that Jones, nice as he was, wasn't for her. Swallow was her pony.

CHAPTER TWO

Jones walked calmly at Wilfred's side and Swallow jogged along beside him, rather more excited now that he was heading for home, or perhaps excited by the strange pony. Rowan tried not to hold on to his mouth, but sometimes he felt as if he would overtake if she gave him his head. She could not help feeling slightly worried, but when Charlie glanced across and said, 'OK?' she answered firmly, 'Yes, thank you.'

Charlie's mind was obviously on his luck in acquiring a free pony. He whistled as they came up over the brow of the down on the same track they had travelled on before. The wind was at their backs and the sun in their eyes, and High Hawes lay below again in the curving arm of the oak wood. Wilfred's long stride took him down easily, Charlie holding him together so that he did not sprawl, and Jones jogged at his side. Swallow tossed his head and snatched at the reins holding his mouth, and started to trot.

'Whoa, Swallow! Don't!'

Rowan heard how feeble she sounded and was ashamed, biting her tongue. It was awful trotting downhill; she was thrown all over the place, and all the time Swallow kept putting his head down by his knees, snatching at her hands. If she held on he nearly pulled her over his head.

'Sit back, Rowan!' she heard Charlie shout. He sounded as worried as she felt. If she sat back she had to let the reins run when Swallow snatched, then he tossed his head up and she had miles of flapping rein and no control at all. It all seemed to be getting worse rather than better.

At the same unfortunate moment, the younger Hawes, released from the dentist, came cantering out of the wood below, first Hugh on Cascade, then Lizzie on Fable and Shrimp on Snowball. Rowan saw Hugh stand up in his stirrups and his shout came thinly on the wind: 'Beat you to the sarsen stone!' They were still far below and hadn't seen the riders above them. Charlie let out a bellow of warning. How did he know Swallow would take off? Rowan wondered, even as her pony's ears disappeared from view and he gave one of his characteristic bucks. By a miracle she survived the buck, but there was no way she could stop the ensuing gallop. Going downhill was terrible. She remembered that she saw Hugh look up and see her, and start to pull Cascade to a skidding halt. She lost one stirrup and then the other and her reins were all tangled up in Swallow's flying mane; the ground flew past beneath her and a terrible fear started to make a strangling feeling in her throat. Her seat was hopelessly insecure. She felt herself rolling and slipping, first to one side and then the other. One more buck would finish it. It came. Rowan went flying and hit the turf a terrific smack, then went rolling over and over down the hill until she came up hard against a rock and hit her head.

So that was what seeing stars meant! It was true. Silver slivers of light splintered her vision, so that nothing else came into focus. She felt intense pain and couldn't see anybody, yet she was aware of action all round her and voices like needles through her skull.

'Take these horses— '

'Charlie, you idiot! You said she wasn't to ride Swallow— '

'Where's that roan beast come from?'

'Is she dead?'

'No, she's moving. Just get those ponies away.'

'Take Swallow, Hugh – what a pig! I think he needs shooting.' That was Shrimp.

'Just clear off home all of you. One of you

hurry on and tell Mum to get the Land-Rover up here.'

After a lot of argument there was silence, only the thud of departing hooves in the grass under Rowan's ear. In the quiet, she thought she was probably all right, only she couldn't move or say anything. Amongst the silver glitter in her vision she saw fragments of Charlie's face, looking like a picture on television when it was a prisoner or someone who mustn't be identified.

'Jeez, Rowan, I'm sorry – it was all my fault. Can you hear me? Do say you're all right!'

'Yes,' she whispered.

She couldn't help it but she felt two large warm tears run down her cheeks, one on either side. It was Shrimp saying Swallow should be shot. Why was she so hopeless, that she couldn't ride him?

'Oh, don't be upset, Rowan. I'm sure it's OK. Can you move your legs? Say something!'

She moved her legs. They felt like lead. Then, to please him she said, 'Swallow.'

It seemed a bit easier now. 'Don't shoot him.'

'No, of course not. We'll work on him, teach him manners. I shouldn't have let you ride him out – I was really stupid. I'm sorry!'

After some minutes the stars stopped blipping

in her vision and she began to feel much less close to death. 'I think I'm all right.' The relief on Charlie's face, now coming into focus like a real face, was evident. 'Thank God for that! You had me really scared. No, don't sit up. Just rest till Ma comes.'

She could think of worse things now, than lying on the warm turf with Charlie beside her. He sat picking nervously at the grass, his earlier good humour overtaken by a darker mood. 'I can't see how I'm going to get by at this new game, if I can't even take a ride out without a casualty. Ma will be furious. I should have left Jones, or whatever he's called, and gone back for him with the trailer.'

He seemed determined that it was his fault, although Rowan was convinced it was her feeble riding that had caused the trouble. When Joan Hawes came rolling across the down in the Land-Rover she obviously agreed with Charlie, for she gave him an icy dressing-down before getting him to lift Rowan into the back of the Land-Rover.

'Bolting ponies are a great advertisement, I must say! I thought we'd agreed nobody was to ride Swallow save Hugh?'

Rowan gave Charlie an anguished look. She thought of Swallow as hers, although she knew

28

perfectly well he wasn't, and the thought of Hugh taking him over really upset her. If he was the pony she was convinced he was, Hugh would never give him up, not when he started winning. Charlie knew what she was thinking.

He said crossly, 'For now – but Rowan will learn. She's not a wimp.'

When they got back to the yard Hugh and Lizzie and Shrimp had put away Wilfred and Swallow, tied up Jones awaiting further instructions, and were ready to start off on their ride again. Hugh looked in and said, 'It's OK. She's still alive.' Then he ran up behind his pony Cascade and jumped on over his hindquarters in his showing-off way. Cascade put back his ears but did not budge: a stocky white pony built like a small tank. He had as much spirit and talent as his rider; they were a well-matched pair. They were Pony Club stars, although Hugh affected to despise Pony Club – 'all those girls.' Rowan guessed that if he couldn't beat the girls, he would stop going. Boys were like that. In spite of Charlie's kind words, she felt she was definitely in the category of wimpy girls. Lizzie, two years older than Hugh and much nicer, said kindly to Rowan, 'Anyone would've fallen off, Rowan – that buck! I would. He's really beastly, that pony.'

She meant it as comfort, but it wasn't much, although Rowan raised a sickly smile. Lizzie got back on Fable, who was a dear: a well-bred, light bay mare with black points, the one anybody could ride. Lizzie, although a very good rider, had been glad to see the back of her old pony, Birdie, an idiosyncratic thoroughbred who had been sold to the show-jumping girl, Matty Prebble. She had appropriated the gentle Fable with relief. Not everybody wanted to show off like Hugh.

They all wanted to know who Jones was and why, so Charlie explained that to them, and they put him out in the field and rode away, and Charlie and his mother took Rowan into the kitchen and sat her down tenderly in Fred Hawes' old armchair.

'I shall have to ring your mother and tell her what's happened,' Joan said. 'You must be checked out after a fall like that. You might be concussed.'

Rowan nearly said, 'Like last time,' then remembered she hadn't told anyone how ill she had felt for a week after banging her head the first time (another of Swallow's bucks).

'Must you tell her?' Charlie asked, echoing Rowan's own feelings. 'You know how anti-horse her dad is.'

'Yes, I must. I'm sorry. You should have thought this through before you put her on Swallow. You've got to learn, Charlie. The hard way, by the look of it.'

Josephine came in while Joan Hawes was telephoning and, seeing Rowan's wan face, and the egg-like lump that was fast emerging over one eye, wanted to know what had happened. Her reaction was not unlike her mother's.

'Oh really, Charlie, you're an absolute idiot.'

'Don't you start! The pony was as good as gold until the last mile when that brainless goon Hugh burst out of the wood at flat gallop. And Rowan sat it very well – the first buck, fine. It was just bad luck she came off.'

'His bucks are dynamite. I think he needs a bullet.'

'Oh, shut up!'

Rowan was mortified by putting Charlie in such a predicament – all her fault that the whole family was castigating poor Charlie, because she was so hopeless! Joan Hawes came back from the phone and told Rowan her mother was coming up to fetch her in the car.

'Just as I thought – she said your father would be annoyed. I don't think he thinks we're a very good influence, after your nice London friends.' But she smiled encouragingly. 'Never mind, Rowan. We'll see that you never have to ride that pony again.'

The last words she wanted to hear! She bit her lip, and saw Charlie's eyes on her, contrite, but he didn't say anything. She sensed that Joan was crosser with Charlie than she wanted to reveal in front of Rowan: she had a very firm set to her lips and her eyes could be flinty at times. She looked haggard since her husband's death, and almost ten years older. Her mother remarked on this fact as she drove Rowan home.

'She does look ill! What a situation to be in – that place to run and all those children – I don't know how they'll keep their heads above water. Especially if they do stupid things like this. I thought you could ride now, Rowan?'

Her father said exactly the same thing, but with rather more heat. 'I've paid over a hundred pounds so far to that place to teach you to ride! What's wrong with them? Or is it you?'

'They didn't *want* the money!' Rowan cried out angrily. 'You made them take it. Of course I can't ride properly yet – it takes years!'

He had been so effusive, pressing the £10 notes on Hugh and Lizzie, which were still pushed, unappreciated, into an instant coffee jar behind the wormers in the tack room. He never understood that they were teaching her as a friend, for fun. Everything was money to him, Rowan supposed, because he was an accountant. He had very odd ideas, as he now started to prove.

'Surely to learn the basics of riding, so that you don't fall off, can be covered in the amount of lessons you've had? I'm not expecting you to jump an Olympic course, just stay on safely. What is so difficult about it? I can't see that family making much of a living if they can't din that much into you.'

Rowan felt it best not to say anything. But after she had seen the doctor and been told to rest at home for a couple of days to counter a hint of concussion, her father had another outbreak of high-mindedness and said she was not to ride again.

'It's too dangerous, and I don't think consorting with a load of gypsies is doing you any good.'

At this Rowan burst into tears and screamed at him, her mother became highly indignant and started to shout, and a family drama erupted. Rowan had noticed that her parents had been having a lot of rows lately but this one, instigated by herself, was a real corker. She retired to her bedroom and neither of them noticed her go. She lay on her bed and sobbed, and her head throbbed, and the row below continued unabated until she fell asleep. She could not believe she wouldn't be allowed to go up to High Hawes again. If her father insisted on the ban, she thought she might as well die. She hiccupped herself to sleep and slept heavily.

When she awoke in the morning it was very quiet and there was no sound of her father getting up and going to work, although it was time. He drove up to the motorway and commuted to London every day, although to Rowan it felt as if London was on a different planet. It certainly was quite a long way. Sometimes, in fact, quite a lot lately, he didn't come home at all. He was always saying how much it cost them, living so far out in the country. Rowan had always shut her ears to this. She thought her father was a pain.

She had rather thought her mother would bring her up a cup of tea and be all sympathetic, but nothing happened, so she got up and got dressed. She felt all right save the egg on her forehead which looked weird and was going purple. Quite a few bits of her were going purple. She felt terribly stiff. She went downstairs and found her mother sitting alone in the kitchen in her dressing-gown, doing nothing. This was unheard of. She didn't even have a cup of tea by her. She was just staring into space. Her face was white and peculiar-looking.

'What's the matter?' Rowan asked.

'Your father's gone.'

'To work?'

'No. Gone. He says he's not coming back.'

Rowan wasn't quite sure how to take this. Her first thought was hooray, now I can still go up to High Hawes. But when she looked at her mother again she saw that this was a very wicked thought and it was quite serious. The phrase 'one-parent family' came into her head. (At least it was the right one parent . . . she had always got on well with her mother.) Then she felt a bit peculiar too, like her mother looked, and sat down opposite her.

There was a long silence between them.

Then Rowan said, 'He'll come back, I should think. When he's cooled down.'

And her mother said, 'No. I don't think he will.'

And he didn't.

CHAPTER THREE

'Both our families have had bad shocks, losing their fathers,' Joan Hawes said to Rowan's mother. 'The best thing the children can do is go off to Pony Club camp and enjoy themselves.'

'I don't know if I can afford it now.'

'You can use the money out of the coffee jar. We've never spent it,' Lizzie said.

'What money?'

'He – Mr Watkins – kept paying us for giving Rowan lessons. We said we didn't want it but he insisted. There's a hundred pounds.'

'That's splendid,' said Joan Hawes. 'Well done.'

'It won't cover the hire of one of your ponies, surely?'

'Rowan does enough work up here to cover all that. We'll make her work harder!'

'I like it!' Rowan declared. She still wasn't at all sure about camp. She looked doubtfully towards Charlie. 'Who shall I ride?'

'Josephine thinks you ought to try Jones. Lizzie's ridden him in the field and he shows no signs of tanking off or not wanting to leave the others. Lizzie wants to take Fable, Hugh's having Swallow and Shrimp wants to try Pinkie. We can always swap around if it doesn't work out.'

'I've never ridden Jones!'

'I'll give you a lesson on Jones,' Josephine said unexpectedly.

'When?' Rowan quaked. She was very nervous of the severe Josephine.

'In a minute. As soon as we've finished lunch.'

They were all sitting round the kitchen table eating ham and salad and hard-boiled eggs. Rowan's mother had come up and been prevailed upon to stay. Since she had been left alone, three days ago, she had been wandering round in a state of shock, and was only just coming to. Rowan felt much the same, deeply disturbed, as if she had been sitting on a chair that had been snatched from underneath her. It was hard to take in, and each time she came home from High Hawes she expected to see her father's car in the drive but it never was. In a way she felt a sense of relief, seeing the empty drive, but underneath, deep down, she felt outraged that he didn't care enough for her to come home. It was terribly hurtful. Each time this hurt came, she turned her brain back to High Hawes and made it concentrate on her luck, not on the family disaster. At least her mother was never going to stop her going up to High Hawes. Hugh said fathers leaving was very common. Rowan said she supposed it wasn't as bad as him dying, like Hugh's father, but it did seem rather weird to think that her father was still around, but not connected with them any more. Her mother hadn't worked since she had married – when she had been her father's secretary. She was now saying she would have to get a job, and looking rather hopeless.

Rowan had always wished her mother was slightly less feeble and more rocklike, like Joan Hawes. Her mother, whose name was Pauline, was much prettier and smarter than Joan Hawes, but Joan Hawes gave off an aura of strength and total reliability that Rowan found very reassuring. She was a big, untidy woman with a majestic posture, rather slow-moving, but a wizard at producing meals from nowhere and saying the right thing at the right time.

'You needn't worry about looking for a job while camp is on. You'll be asked to help with the catering – that'll keep your mind off your troubles for a week. We can go over together. You'll meet a lot of nice people.'

'I haven't really met anybody since I came to live here.'

'No, you don't unless you join things. We don't go out of our way to be friendly, on the whole. But if you're in trouble, you'll find people will come out of the woodwork.'

Rowan felt very good about her mother being friends with Joan Hawes, less good about her lesson with Josephine.

'Go and tack him up. We'll sort you out.'

Rowan did as she was told. She wished desperately it was Charlie. Everything was fun with Charlie, but Josephine was a serious girl, and did not smile a lot. She was tall and rather beautiful in her cool blonde way and, although they were so different, was very close to Charlie since the two of them had taken on the brunt of running High Hawes to make a livelihood. Rowan had noticed how it was weighing on them.

Josephine said, 'You've got to get to know this pony, and I've got to practise my teaching.' She even smiled. Rowan felt better.

She found Jones very nice to ride, obedient and comfortable, and able to understand her inexperienced demands. He didn't give her the feeling that disaster was imminent, as Swallow did, that she was tiptoeing round the edge of a sleeping volcano. He was laid-back but not unwilling, and Josephine taught her how to try and collect him so that he held himself together when he trotted, but admitted that it wasn't easy for a beginner. 'You do it with your back and leg muscles, and these have to develop. The "seat" is everything, and it takes a long time to develop it.'

Rowan was not encouraged, feeling she had started too late. But Josephine laughed at her fears and said, 'You have the right attitude, that's what matters. Hugh, for example, thinks he knows it all. He can ride Swallow's bucks, no trouble, but he has no finesse. One day he will find out.'

'Has Charlie got finesse?' Rowan dared to ask.

Josephine said crossly, 'Oh, Charlie's got everything. I hate him!' But then she smiled. 'It's no good trying to copy Charlie. He does it by instinct. He can't teach to save his life because he can't understand why other people can't get the same results as he does.'

'But I thought High Hawes was going to be a riding school and Charlie is going to be a teacher?'

'It's not going to work out that way.'

'Charlie said— '

'Charlie doesn't know!' Rowan got the impression that Josephine was crying out to her what she hadn't voiced to anybody else – the worries that kept her tight and silent and depressed. Her cool look was suddenly quite passionate. 'Charlie knows he doesn't like teaching but he doesn't understand why. It'll never work – Charlie teaching children. And me – I'm not a lot better. I haven't got the right temperament to be a teacher. I get cross if people are stupid, instead of laughing and making it fun. It isn't fun, to me. It's deadly serious.'

'But how can you start up a riding school with no-one who can teach?'

'Exactly,' said Josephine. 'That's what keeps me awake at nights.'

Rowan was amazed at Josephine's confidences. She suspected that they had not been voiced to anyone else in the family and Josephine confirmed this by adding, as they went to put Jones away, 'Don't tell the others any of this. I always worry about things. I can't help it. I might have it all wrong.'

Rowan said, 'I think you're a good teacher. I think that was the best lesson I've ever had. Better than with any of the others.'

And Josephine said, 'Yes. That's because

you think the same as me. You're deadly serious too.'

Rowan was astonished.

*　　*　　*

There were forty applicants for Pony Club camp. The only others Rowan knew besides the Hawes were Barbara Bailey, the farmer's daughter who lived just along the road from her, and Matty Prebble, the show-jumping girl – although she only knew her a bit, by sight. Barbara was known as Babar the Elephant by the Hawes (she was a large girl and did not mind, Babar being such a nice character). In spite of her laid-back manner, broad speech and bun face she was brilliant at school and knocked spots off all of them. She had a weedy old pony called Black Diamond who couldn't do anything, and lately, since Charlie had bought the job-lot of riding school ponies, she had taken to riding the chestnut cob, Armchair. She had found the difference, after Diamond, amazing and was now torn with guilt at preferring Armchair over poor old Diamond.

'I would love to take Armchair to camp,' she confided to Rowan, 'but I can't abandon poor Diamond.'

'Ask Charlie what he thinks.'

Charlie said, 'Yes, take the Armchair. It will do him good – and you. You'll have far more fun on him than on Diamond. If you like, Diamond can come up here, and we can use him for nervous pupils – if we get any, that is. He can earn his keep.'

Babar's large round face lit up at this. 'That would be great! I don't want 'im to think I don't love 'im any more.'

'Horses don't get huffy, like human beings,' Charlie said.

'He likes it up 'ere, because of the company. 'E's only got cows at home.'

'That's it then. Everyone's happy.'

Rowan knew Charlie would solve it. The pressure on Babar's loyalty was dissolved and she started to take a more proprietary interest in the Armchair, grooming him diligently and schooling him over small jumps. She had never been able to get Diamond to jump even a cavalletti. The Armchair was a very amiable animal, no oil-painting, but a rather flash bright chestnut, fourteen-and-a-half hands high, with stout legs and hairy heels, a hogged flaxen mane and a bushy, unmanageable cream tail. Rowan had once seen Josephine riding him and had been surprised how very smartly he went and how good he looked, almost like a show cob. She did not know that a sign of a good rider was not necessarily how they handled the difficult horses, but how they made the slugs perform. Not that the Armchair was a slug, but he didn't look quite the same for Babar as he did for a talented Hawes. Babar's enthusiasm for camp, now she had a new horse, inspired Rowan to rather more enthusiasm herself. There was only a week to go, and she got out her list of instructions to make sure she would be well prepared.

She was to be in Orange Ride and share accommodation with a girl called Roma Glade. 'Roma Glade' conjured up a rather dreary vision in Rowan's mind; it sounded like an air freshener.

'Never heard of her,' said Hugh. He then went on to explain that the Orange Ride was for older but fairly useless riders. 'Green Ride is for younger but better riders. Blue Ride is top, Red Ride second top. I'm in Red. I should be in Blue really, but I'm too young. Shrimp's in Green. Lizzie's in Red with me.'

Lizzie said, 'Don't take any notice of him. Orange is not for "fairly useless riders" – it's for people without a lot of experience. And it's only rough anyway – nearly everyone complains they're in the wrong ride. Hugh can't believe he's not in the top ride – he has to say it's because he's too young, but Charlie was in the top ride when he was eleven.'

'He didn't have a difficult pony like Cascade,' Hugh said hotly.

'His pony didn't have a duff rider like you!'

'I don't stand a chance of winning anything on Swallow anyway.'

'Poor diddums!'

At this point Shrimp came in and stopped the conversation by saying, rather tearfully, she didn't see how she could take Pinkie away to camp for a week without taking Bonzo too, as Bonzo was now so attached to his surrogate 'mother' Pinkie that he would pine if she went away. 'He'll have to come too. I still have to feed him anyway, and Ma won't want to do it for a week.'

Bonzo was Shrimp's orphan foal which she had hand-fed since birth. It was now a very pushy colt of two months, turned out with the little strawberry roan mare Pinkie to whom he had struck up a fierce attachment. Pinkie was another of Charlie's bargain buys, having been discarded for a knee injury, but the injury had cleared up completely with rest. Shrimp, who had always ridden show-ponies for professional show-people and never had her own pony, now lavished attention on her two darlings, Bonzo and Pinkie, as if to make up all the time she had lost out in the family, being away at shows.

Apparently 'Auntie Millie' gave permission for Bonzo to come too, for when the morning arrived when they all set off to ride over the down to camp, he was let out to run free behind the group of ponies. Children and ponies were all unrecognizably smart. The children sported snow-white shirts and gleaming badges, well-brushed jackets and spotless jods, and the ponies shone, their manes and tails freshly washed and hooves polished. Rowan could not keep her eyes off Swallow, whose blue-black coat showed faint dapples across the belly, chinking his bit against Hugh's restraining hand. He looked like a little fairy-tale charger, all spirit and strength, tossing the heavy forelock with impatience.

Charlie's instructions were to walk all the way, fiercely reiterated to Hugh. Babar was in charge, riding the Armchair. For once her gumboots had been replaced by proper riding-boots, and her mothy anorak by an equally ancient but correct tweed jacket. Following her through the wood, watching Swallow, Rowan was relieved to be on sensible Jones and for the first time felt a slight optimism about the week ahead. Her mother, still in a state of shock and frequently in tears, had cheered up notably at the prospect of the hard work in the catering department that awaited her over at Sand House, the abode of Jeremy Patterson. Jerry was now thankfully defecting to High Hawes for the week. Joan Hawes and Pauline were driving over with all their children's gear to see them settled in, and Josephine and Charlie would follow in the Land-Rover after lunch, when their services would be required.

The ride to Sand House was uneventful, due to the firm restraining influence of Lizzie and Babar on Hugh who, in spite of instructions, kept suggesting 'a nice canter'. Although kept under restraint, he didn't sulk, just laughed, which was the nice thing about him and why, although he was so horrid, one couldn't help liking him. Rowan rode along thinking how incredibly lucky she was to have fallen in with this amazing family and nice Babar, when she could have been marooned at home all the holidays with her neurotic mother. And her mother too, taken in hand by Joan Hawes, turned cheerful when she came up to High Hawes, and was really keen to start cooking Pony Club dinners. Rowan had a bit of a guilt feeling then, about thinking herself lucky when her father had left them to run off with his secretary, but she couldn't help how she felt.

Certainly she missed him, but mostly it was a relief to be free of his bad temper. Perhaps now he was with his secretary he was all smiles.

'Put Bonzo on a lead-rope,' Babar commanded, as they came down the track to join the road. Horse-boxes and trailers were approaching the drive to Sand House, and cars full of gear, stirring up the somnolent valley. It was a hazy, close day, and their ties felt hot – Hugh had pulled his apart and rode with his jacket flapping open. Swallow had behaved like a lamb all the way, Rowan noticed crossly. She felt very nervous as they crossed the road and followed an enormous cream horse-box up the drive, choking in its dust.

'That's Priscilla Hicks,' Hugh said, and made his being-sick face. 'She's never come to camp before because her horse is too valuable to come slumming. But now Auntie Millie has collared Jerry's yard, she thinks she'll honour us with her presence.'

Behind them the Prebbles' equally large box, driven by a groom, throttled down, deciding not to overtake. They pulled off the drive on to the grass verge to let it by, and Rowan saw Matty's pale face looking down at them, unsmiling.

'She's another who's only come because we've got posh stables this year. She never comes ordinarily – not when we were at the farm and the ponies had to be tied up in the cow-byre.

Rowan wondered how big Roma Glade's horse-box would be, as she was going to sleep in it for a week. Priscilla and Matty were going to be in luxury in the living accommodation of their vast horse-boxes; Lizzie and Shrimp were going to share space in one of the few safe dormer rooms over the stables and Hugh was sharing a trailer with a boy called Alan Finch who he said was all right. Just before they reached the stable yard another trailer passed them, this time a very rickety affair pulled by a wheezing Land-Rover. On the trailer's tailboard a notice announced: 'Glade's Pigs. Organic Bacon from Free Range Farms.'

'That's your home!' Hugh shouted with great glee. 'A pig trailer! Jeez, Rowan, I hope they've hosed it out!'

Even the girls thought it was rather funny, so Rowan tried to smile gamely, but her expectations were plummeting by the minute. They turned into the old stable yard, which was now humming with activity. The horse-boxes had driven through it to the far field, where the ponies were being unloaded, and Auntie Millie was inspecting the arrivals under the walnut tree, and allocating stables, helped by Matty's mother, the sharp Mrs Prebble (who was not the most popular mother in Long Bottom) and Jerry Patterson. Rowan was much encouraged by Jerry's smile of recognition.

'So Jones is at work already? Do him the world of good. How do you get on with him?'

'He's lovely.'

Had Jerry heard about her accident with Swallow, she wondered?

'Get off and trot him out for me, will you?'

Rowan got off. She had no idea what she had to do to trot him out, but luckily dear Lizzie saw her hesitation and said quickly, 'I'll go first!' It appeared that one led the pony away up the yard and trotted him back in a straight line, aiming straight at Jerry. This was to make sure no lame ponies were passed in. The stalwart Millie Mildmay watched grimly. She was a four-square, sixtyish woman in a green quilted jacket and fawn trousers, who moved with a strange rolling gait born of many injuries from falls in point-to-points. She had gimlet eyes, a mousetrap mouth, and hairs on her chin. But her dark eyes were full of a zest for living; they raked over Rowan and her pony and came to rest challengingly on Rowan's terrified face.

'Who are you then? You're not a Hawes, are you? Or is my mind going?'

'I'm Rowan Watkins. I ride with them – the Hawes.'

'Ha! Good for you. Run your stirrups up. Never leave them dangling after you've dismounted. How shall we arrange your ponies then? All good friends, are they? Which one is that ridiculous foal attached to?'

Shrimp scowled. Bonzo was a skewbald and did look slightly ridiculous, standing there with his long rabbit ears pricked with surprise at the goings-on, all legs and cheek.

'He'll have to stay shut up while you're riding, for goodness sake. He won't kick the box down, I hope?'

She let out a great guffaw at the idea and clapped the foal on the hindquarters. Shrimp scowled at her and received a beaming smile. 'And you, young lady, we've got to teach you to ride properly, haven't we? No more sitting up there in your red hair ribbons smiling and just looking pretty. Take that foal and your pony to the box in the corner and put the other mare in with them.' She pointed at Fable. 'If you think that's best. You know them better than I do. And you, Rowan, does your pony get on with Hugh's new beast? Will they share?'

'I want to share with Alan Finch,' said Hugh.

Lizzie said, 'Yes. Swallow and Jones are friends.'

'Good. Put them together.' She ignored Hugh. 'And you, Barbara— '

They led their ponies to their boxes. Hugh was furious and Shrimp was almost in tears at the insult to her riding. 'I bet she couldn't show a horse to save her life. She only knows about crashing cross-country and falling off.'

Lizzie said, 'You'll just have to show her then, won't you?'

Shrimp glared at her, even while digesting the truth of her sister's remark. She had something of the same nature as Auntie Millie herself, Rowan thought, remembering the night Bonzo had been born, and her courage in saving him from the berserk dam. Shrimp's week was already set up – to *show* Millie Mildmay. Her eyes were blazing. She was nine, and small for her age, but her character enlarged her presence remarkably. Poor Pinkie was going to have a tough week. The pretty little mare, a pure Welsh mountain, twelve hands high, was already searching the large porcelain manger for signs of sustenance and Bonzo was quickly copying her.

Rowan reckoned she had got off lightly from

the formidable Mrs Mildmay and untacked Jones in his allotted box while Hugh muttered crossly over Swallow. How nice, Rowan was thinking, that she would be sharing the box with dear Swallow. As she slipped off her bridle, Hugh looked out over the door and said, 'There's Princess Priscilla. Look at her! Mummy Prebble's buttering her up, you can see.'

Priscilla Hicks was extraordinarily handsome, along with her young thoroughbred. She had long, red, very curly hair which was immediately eye-catching, and large amber-coloured eyes like a cat's. Rowan was stunned by the elegant, imperious way she stood at her horse's head while Mrs Prebble gushed away. She was said to be sixteen, but had the authority of an adult; her confidence no doubt built upon her arresting beauty. Rowan could not help but admire such a picture, in spite of Hugh's yukking noises. She was what most insignificant mouse-coloured girls like Rowan dreamed they might turn into one day, and knew quite assuredly they would not.

'Daddy Hicks bought that horse for her from Franke Sloothaak. It cost millions.'

'Who's Franke Sloothaak?'

'He's the world champion show-jumper. Well, usually he is. They've only brought it to camp to get it used to going in company and roughing it a bit. Auntie Millie said it's too uptight. She thinks mixing with the likes of us will do it good. Princess Priscilla is having trouble with it, you see.'

Rowan tried to digest that people with 'millions' to spend and with looks like a top model had the same sort of troubles as she did. Difficult. She couldn't see it.

Lizzie said, 'Look at Mrs Prebble! Her darling Matty is always top dog at camp and now Princess Priscilla's decided to come she's going to get her nose put out of joint.' She grinned at Rowan. 'Aren't we catty? The trouble is,' she explained, 'when it comes to being in the teams, we all want to be in the Pony Club team, but people like them take the places. And they aren't real members, doing all the nitty-gritty – they only come to the minimum number of rallies to qualify – they never do any of the fun things, like treasure hunts and tet and things.'

Rowan supposed she would learn what 'tet' was in due course – there was too much to take in all at once. It struck her that a lot of members might think the Hawes were privileged – were they always chosen for the teams? She was sure Charlie and Josephine must have been. On the other hand they did it by sheer hard work – no-one ever bought them expensive ponies.

Even Cascade, the star, had been obtained almost for nothing, as he was considered dangerous.

Jones and Swallow seemed perfectly happy in their shared box, both looking out over the half-door to watch the goings-on in the yard. Nearly everyone else arrived by lorry or trailer, most of which parked in the field beyond the yard to become living accommodation for the week. There was a gate from this field into the garden of the house, where a large mess-tent had been set up for eating in, convenient to the kitchen. The two big fields on either side of the drive, next to the road, were where the riding would take place, and Hugh said there was a cross-country course up the lane a little way in the grounds of a National Trust house. Apparently, such was Auntie Millie's clout, she could arrange these things. The tenant of the house was one of her many relations. Apparently she had twenty-six cousins, mostly horsey.

Princess Priscilla's beautiful horse had been given a loose-box all to himself, where he was tossing himself around in circles and scraping his bedding into heaps. Rowan heard Auntie Millie say to Jerry, 'I think we've all bitten off a bit more than we can chew in that department,' with a nod in the gelding's direction, to which Jerry replied with a grin, 'Pass her over to Charlie. He'll sort her out.'

Rowan felt rather disturbed on Charlie's behalf, and a nasty jealous feeling turned in her stomach, which she squashed by making herself concentrate on Roma Glade, who had just led her pony in from the horse-box field and given her name to Mrs Mildmay. To Rowan's relief she was not in the Princess Priscilla league, but a rather earnest-looking, twelvish girl with untidy hair sticking out from under her hat and an equally earnest-looking pony, a rather stout dun who she said was called Honeypot.

'Right about the pot,' remarked Mrs Mildmay. 'Not very fit, by the look of him. You're sharing with that new girl who came with the Hawes, so you'd better put your pony by theirs, up there. Rowan and Roma – you sound like a circus act, on the trapeze, eh!' She let out one of her bellowing laughs.

'Go and talk to her.' Lizzie gave Rowan a shove.

Hugh marched up beside Rowan and said, 'Hi, Roma. This is Rowan who's going to share your pig-lorry.'

'I scrubbed it out last night, honestly. It doesn't smell of pigs at all, only a bit of him.' She nodded at her pony, and looked dubiously at Rowan.

Hugh marched off to find Alan, Lizzie went to see if Fable was all right, and Roma said to Rowan, 'I was really worried when they told me I was sharing with a Hawes.'

'I'm not a Hawes!'

'You've got a Hawes pony though. It's bound to be brilliant.'

'No. They've only had it a week. All their ponies are new. They're rescued ponies.'

'Hasn't Hugh got Cascade and Lizzie got Birdie?'

'No.'

Roma looked much happier all of a sudden. 'I thought you'd be brilliant like them. Honeypot won't jump, you know. Not even a cavalletti. He just won't. I didn't want to come but my mum made me.'

'I can't jump. I can't even ride, really,' Rowan confessed.

'Oh, good,' said Roma.

They warmed to each other at once after these confessions, and went back to the field to the pig trailer. Joan Hawes and Pauline Watkins had arrived with all their gear and backed up the estate car to unload Rowan's stuff. There was barely room for the two camp-beds side by side, with a little slice at the top for their bag of clothes. They had to sit on the beds as there was no gap between. Pauline looked appalled but Rowan thought it looked very cosy.

'At least we'll have no housework to do,' Roma said. 'We get marked each morning for how tidy it is. Priscilla will have to get the Hoover out to do her floor, and wipe round the fridge every morning! Have you seen her horse? It's called Out of the West, and cost ten thousand pounds.'

Rowan thought Out of the West was a most beautiful name, if not very handy, and couldn't help feeling that the lovely Priscilla was possibly dreading the week ahead even more than she had been. She must know how everyone was gossiping about her. Now it had started, and Roma seemed quite normal, Rowan was beginning to enjoy herself. It was nearly lunchtime and when they had tidied up they had to go back to the yard, and hay and water their ponies under the eagle eye of a fierce girl called Octavia or, more usually, Otty. She was a sort of budding Mrs Mildmay, not yet weathered and lame. She had short, dark hair and a brown face and was very quick and strong.

Roma said, 'I think she might be teaching Orange Ride. I hope so. She's nice.'

Rowan had prayed Orange Ride would get Charlie, but he had been given the top ride with Priscilla, and Matty Prebble. It was all up on a noticeboard outside the mess-tent. Hugh and Lizzie were in Red Ride with Mrs Prebble in charge and Otty was, as Roma surmised, down for Orange. Josephine had Green, which Shrimp was in. Roma said she would have had Red save for Lizzie and Hugh being in it, as apparently it wasn't good to be taught by a relation, if it could be helped. There was only one ride below Orange, called Yellow, which was for very small children. Rowan was relieved to see that there were older (possibly worse?) riders in Orange. She felt much better now she had discovered there were other members as diffident as herself.

They went into the mess-tent and sat down for lunch. It was an easy one of ham, salad, tinned fruit and ice-cream because the kitchen was not yet organized. When they had eaten Mrs Mildmay gave them a harangue about being helpful, manners, behaviour, going to sleep at Lights Out ('Some hope!' Rowan heard Otty remark) and remembering that their ponies deserved the first and best of their time.

After a final glare her face immediately switched to sweetness and light and she let out her great laugh and said, 'Remember, it's fun! Enjoy yourselves!'

They all filed out (except the duty group for the day who had to wash up and clear away) and got their riding clothes and tacked up their ponies. The first afternoon was a sorting out with their instructors. Hugh, tacking up Swallow, was moaning about having Mrs Prebble.

'You're all right – Otty's nice. Mrs Prebble's downright cruel . . . hours of sitting trot and on the bit and stuff. Swallow'll hate it.'

'You will, you mean,' Lizzie said.

Otty had changed from shirt and jeans into pristine jods and boots, white shirt and tie and a jacket. When Rowan led Jones out she saw Charlie talking to Mrs Mildmay. He was dressed similarly, and looked amazing. For a moment she didn't recognize him, not until he turned away and saw her, and grinned. In spite of being told how lucky she was to have Otty for an instructor, Rowan wished desperately she had Charlie. Charlie's ride consisted of six girls of about fifteen; Matty Prebble was the youngest. She rode Birdie, the thoroughbred pony that had once been Lizzie's.

'She's welcome,' Lizzie said, as they watched her mount. Birdie was uptight as usual, spinning round nervously. Charlie went across and held her. Matty scowled furiously and rode away across the yard, out into the field. As soon as she had gone Priscilla came out of her loose-box with Out of the West. Out of the West was sixteen-and-a-half hands high, with an arrogant and commanding outlook that made him seem bigger. He was beautifully made, up to weight, and very eye-catching with his gleaming black coat. Rowan saw the look on Charlie's face, of pure admiration. She hoped it was for the horse, and not its rider, who had an instinctive way of looking at the opposite sex, with a bold come-hither smile and then a lowering of the eyes and a flutter of the long dark lashes. Rowan, staring, was terribly impressed.

'Get a move on, Rowan,' Otty said.

The five rides were marked out in the two flat fields on either side of the drive with coloured cones, and the riders went to their colour and lined up to have their tack examined by their instructor. If it was all new to Rowan, it was obvious that most children knew the drill. There was plenty of laughing and teasing, save – noticeably – in Mrs Prebble's ride. Otty was kindly and not over-critical, and Rowan was confident that her pony and tack were in good order and had no worries. It was the actual riding she was nervous of, of not being good enough.

But she need not have worried. To her astonishment she found there was nothing that she couldn't cope with, and at the end of the afternoon Otty said to her, 'Well done, Rowan. You've made a good start.'

Rather different from Hugh, to whom Mrs Prebble was saying in her acid voice, 'I don't know why you bother to come when you make it so apparent you know everything.'

Lizzie said to Rowan, 'Her own darling daughter was having trouble with Birdie, did you notice? She could see, out of the corner of her eye. It's made her terribly cross. I'm so glad it's Matty on Birdie, and not me any more. Fable's a darling.'

Rowan was surprised how hungry she was when they went in for tea.

CHAPTER FOUR

Rowan adored this new, strange life: sleeping in the pig-trailer; getting up at midnight to trail across the moonlit field to giggle and trade crisps with two others of their ride living in comparative splendour in a caravan; dodging the night patrol by rolling into a ditch (dry fortunately) and overhearing a gem of gossip from the lips of Auntie Millie herself as she walked past with Otty: 'I'm afraid Lucy Prebble is very unsuited to Pony Club life. She's a pain, and I'm sorry for the children who have to bear with her. But it's difficult to give volunteers the sack. We just have to make the best of it.'

To this Otty replied, 'According to Charlie, Matty Prebble's not getting on very well with that new pony of hers. If she's having trouble, Mrs Prebble will be upset and that makes her temper worse.'

They walked on, and Rowan and Roma went on lying in the ditch for a bit, to be on the safe side. The friends in the caravan had given them a glass of cider each, and Rowan was impressed by how the stars were circling round the sky and how the ditch seemed to swing gently like a hammock, so that it was more comfortable to stay than to go. It was very warm, and the dark downs seemed to wrap them round in a friendly fashion. Rowan felt fantastically, incredibly happy.

Roma said, 'It's a bit embarrassing for your Haweses if they sold Birdie to the Prebbles and she's no good.'

Rowan said, 'Mrs Prebble insisted on having her. She answered the ad. She tried to beat the price down, but Charlie wouldn't. He didn't hide anything about Birdie. She *is* a difficult pony. That's why Lizzie didn't like her. But Mrs Prebble knew all that. I suppose she thought Matty was good enough to cope with her.'

'It's funny', Roma said, 'how some ponies are just right for a person, and all wrong for another. I don't think Honeypot is right for me somehow. Or perhaps it's just me.'

'Yes, I think that.' Rowan knew Jones was right for her, but she wanted Swallow. Lizzie wanted to keep Fable although her family scorned her lack of ambition. Hugh and Cascade were made for each other. Rowan thought of dear Swallow in his mahogany-lined stable, picking at his haynet. 'I *will* ride him!' she whispered to herself. She looked up at the sharp half-circle of a sickle moon lying above the downs and made a fierce vow. Roma had got up and walked on and Rowan supposed she had to go too, but for a moment it was the most important thing in the world, to lie in the ditch committing herself to dear Swallow. Roma came back, rather worried.

'Are you all right?'

'Oh, yes!'

It was all to do with being so lucky and so happy, not living in Putney any more but having landed up with the Haweses, and having Jones to ride and Swallow to aspire to. She got up and started back for the pig-trailer behind Roma.

'Swallow was stolen, you know, and nobody really knows who owns him properly.'

'What are you talking about?'

Rowan couldn't remember.

The next day Mrs Prebble picked a row with Charlie, accusing him of upsetting Matty by his 'inadequate teaching'. She said to Mrs Mildmay, 'He's too young and totally unqualified to teach a Pony Club top ride.'

Auntie Millie stuck out her famous jaw. 'Yes, you're right. But I have faith in him. I don't think the trouble lies with Charlie. I think it lies with Matty.'

'Then I'll have her in my ride and sort her out myself.'

'Yes. Try it.'

Mrs Mildmay asked Lizzie to go and tell Charlie she wanted him. The rides were just preparing to go out, and he was giving Priscilla a leg up on Out of the West. They were laughing together and Rowan, hearing them, felt a stab of the old familiar jealousy. Charlie was hers! Was Auntie Millie going to tell him off?

He came over, looking slightly nervous.

'Mrs Prebble is going to take Matty into her own ride. She's not satisfied with your teaching.'

Charlie did not look too worried.

'Am I supposed to be upset?'

'No. I just want your side of the story.'

'Matty doesn't get on with Birdie. She hypes her up and Birdie's losing her confidence. The more Matty has a go at her, the more Birdie decides she doesn't like it. They give her too much hard feed and they haven't let her out in a field since they bought her. What do they expect?'

'Have you told Mrs Prebble this?'

'I'm not daft! I've told Matty. I've tried to get her to relax, let the mare down, stop over-feeding her, not ask too much of her.

They've only had her three weeks and the mare needs sympathy, not force.'

'You sold the pony to them. Did it occur to you she might not suit?'

'I advertised the mare for sale and Mrs Prebble answered the ad. Dad always knew she wanted her, because of the jump she's got, but I purposely didn't offer her to Mrs Prebble because she's such a pain, and when it comes to show-jumping, she asks such a lot of youngsters. You know Dad didn't worry about things like that if the money was offered. But Mrs Prebble turned up and haggled, and when I refused she coughed up the price. What could I do?'

Mrs Mildmay frowned.

Charlie said, rather tentatively, 'It's difficult for me, having sold them the mare. But I think they're going to have trouble if they carry on the way they are. It could be dangerous.'

'But Lizzie rode Birdie. You didn't think she was dangerous then, surely?'

'No. Lizzie was nervous of Birdie, that's why she didn't want to keep her. But she was never dangerous. We didn't keep her hyped up like the Prebbles do and Lizzie tried to keep her calm. Perhaps you could tell them to cool it a bit, take their time? It's no good my saying anything.'

'I think I agree with you, my lad. I'll see what I can do.' She looked far from confident. 'Pity. How are you getting on with Miss Hicks? Or should I say her horse?'

Charlie flushed up slightly. 'Her horse is magnificent. Much too strong for her. Heaven only knows what will happen when she takes him cross-country.'

'Well, I must say, you fill me with confidence! I think I'll go and check up on our insurance policies.'

Charlie laughed.

Rowan overheard a lot of this while she was tightening her girths and waiting for Roma on the plodding Honeypot. They rode together out to their orange markers in the field and Otty told them they were going to ride along the road to the cross-country course and hack through the woods, up and down banks, across ditches and over a few logs. This caused a fair amount of panic amongst the motley members of the Orange ride, although Rowan felt quite happy about it. Otty led the way on a cob called Ben which she had 'borrowed'. Its rider had been sick in the night and deflected into 'Welfare', a sagging tent with two moth-eaten camp-beds in it.

The road led up a narrowing valley where the downs rose up steeply on either side. It was hot and sleepy out of the wind and the ponies clattered along behind Ben. Roma was complaining to Rowan, 'Honeypot won't jump a thing, nor a ditch either. I shall be useless doing this. I should have gone sick like Tracy.'

After half a mile, the land on the left side of the road flattened out and became the old parkland of the National Trust house. The parkland merged into woodland and Rowan could see the jumps the Pony Club fathers had built: some island jumps in the grass and then others leading into the woods.

'We'll never jump those!' Roma muttered.

The Red ride was already circling on the parkland. They were using the Hunter Trial course for that session and Mrs Prebble shouted imperiously to Otty to make sure she didn't get her children in the way. She turned away and Otty stuck her tongue out. Rowan could see dear Swallow lined up with Hugh on board, and Lizzie on Fable and, at the top of the row, Matty on the sweating Birdie. Even Rowan, with no experience, could see that Birdie was far more of a handful for Matty than she had ever been back home when Lizzie rode her. She would not stand still, but pranced and swung round and tossed her head. Matty was red-faced and cross. Hugh sat on the immobile Swallow watching her with his usual expression of smug conceit.

Mrs Prebble wanted them all to jump a log that had blown over from the edge of the woodland. It was huge at one end and quite low at the other. They all went over one by one, mostly in the middle, but when it was Hugh's turn he put Swallow into a fast canter and turned him for the largest part of the jump. Rowan's heart missed a beat as she watched. But she might have known . . . Hugh was a true Hawes, and Swallow jumped perfectly, ridden with such confidence and skill. Rowan was thrilled – not so Mrs Prebble, who scolded Hugh angrily for showing off. Hugh just smiled. When it was Birdie's turn, she got so steamed up that she refused twice, and then tried to run away after cat-hopping awkwardly over the lowest part.

Otty smiled and said, 'Poor Mrs Prebble!' Her eyes gleamed.

They rode into the parkland and Otty took them down the far end away from Mrs Prebble's voice and lined them up to jump a very modest log, all of nine inches high. Some of the ponies took it in a trotting stride; Jones gave a beautiful little jump and Rowan managed to stay in place, then Honeypot waddled up to it and stopped dead.

While Otty went to sort him out, Rowan went into a dream of flying over jumps on

Swallow, looking for the highest part. She would lie up with her hands up his neck whispering encouragement into his lovely little ears and he would jump for his team . . . for his country . . . for silver cups as high as your chest . . .

'Get off, Rowan, and let Roma have a try on Jones.'

Roma was nearly in tears. She gathered up Jones's reins, muttering, 'I could *kill* Honeypot.'

'You get up on Honeypot, Rowan, and see if you can make him jump,' Otty said.

Honeypot only wanted to graze. Rowan felt it was like sitting on a barrel, and the feeling of approaching the log at a sluggish trot and slowing to an irrevocable walk and a halt just as he got there was very depressing.

Otty got impatient and said, 'We can't spend all day with him, Roma, I'm afraid. You'll just have to have turns on the others.'

They changed back and Rowan realized once more how lucky she was. Jones was an obliging pony and never gave her frights. She thoroughly enjoyed scrambling through the woods, over banks and ditches and the odd small logs. He was the best pony by far and made it easy for her. Some of the others wouldn't go over ditches nor through a small stream, and Honeypot wouldn't do anything. Roma cried. Otty succeeded in getting the others round, but not Roma. Rowan lent her Jones again to cheer her up and rode Honeypot back to the park with the others along a peaty ride. She wondered if Charlie could make him jump the log, or even Hugh.

They came to a well-built jump which gave onto the ride and, hearing crashing noises and screams approaching through the wood, they pulled rather nervously into a clearing to wait. In a moment a bay pony appeared, very fast and looking largely out of control. Rowan recognized Birdie at once, her long ears flitching wildly and her eyes frightened. Matty was riding hard, looking very tense. The jump was solid, made of telegraph poles, but it wasn't very high. Birdie straightened up for it, saw it, and at the last moment refused, digging in her feet and tearing long streamers out of the peat. Matty screamed at her and gave her a huge belt with her whip behind the saddle, at which Birdie jumped wildly from a standstill. She caught her front feet against the log, being in too close, and turned a mighty somersault, flying through the air and landing with a flump in the middle of the ride. Matty was thrown clear, but Birdie, trying to scramble to her feet, slipped on the wet leaf-mould and fell again, heavily, on her side, on top of Matty.

Matty screamed. Birdie flailed wildly, lurched up and galloped away through the trees.

Matty lay still.

The members of the Orange ride were, for a moment, too terrified to move. The wood was suddenly immensely silent, all the action stilled. The sun filtered down through the trees, making patterns across the ride, and a thrush was singing serenely as if nothing had happened. Rowan stared at Matty's sprawled figure, expecting every second to see it move, but nothing happened. She got off Honeypot, as no-one else seemed to be doing anything, and started to walk towards Matty. She felt very sick.

Matty lay on her front with her arms flung out, her face buried in the earth. There was no blood or anything but somehow, to Rowan, there was an intangible indication of seriousness about her position that was terrifying. One of the others shouted at Rowan, 'You aren't supposed to move them!' She knew that.

While she was standing there she heard suddenly a steady thrumming of hooves from behind. It was too late to stop anybody, so she just had to turn round and stand in front of Matty to protect her. She looked up and saw Swallow approaching, head up, ears pricked.

'Hugh! Stop!' she screamed.

She saw Hugh's face above Swallow's streaming mane, very cool. He steered into the corner of the jump and jumped very neatly, well clear of Matty, and pulled up at once.

'Jeez, what's happened?'

'Birdie fell on her!'

'Serves her right,' Hugh said. 'I'll go and fetch her ma.'

He wheeled round and galloped full pelt away down the ride towards the park. The others pulled themselves together and posted someone to stop further riders, and someone cantered back to fetch Otty, and soon Rowan was no longer alone with the casualty. Otty arrived, and Mrs Prebble herself came storming along on a borrowed pony. Hugh came back and said to Rowan, 'I'm going to look for poor Birdie. Coming?'

'Yes.'

Rowan was thankful to have a job to do, and pleased that Hugh had asked her. They followed the Hunter Trial course and Hugh jumped the jumps. Rowan went round. She felt a bit queasy and cold, and couldn't take pleasure now in watching Swallow, unnerved by Matty's so-sudden demise.

They found Birdie in the far corner of the wood, grazing, her reins tangled up under her legs. Hugh got off and sorted her out, talking to her kindly. She was sweating and very nervous.

'They've ruined her,' he said. 'Mrs Prebble is really stupid. She goes on and on at Matty.'

Rowan sat on the solid Honeypot, holding Swallow's reins. Swallow rubbed his nose against her knee. Hugh loosened Birdie's girths, and stroked her sweaty neck.

'The trouble is, they'll blame us. I bet you. They'll say Birdie is dangerous. Probably want their money back.'

He got back on Swallow, and Birdie walked between them, quiet now, as if she recognized she was back with friends. Rowan felt better, calmed by Hugh's calming of Birdie. He wasn't the big-headed Hugh now, but the nicer boy that was sometimes seen lurking underneath. How strange it was, Rowan thought, how different it was for everybody with their ponies – Roma crying because she couldn't jump a twig, Matty being pushed by her dreadful mother, Priscilla having the best that money could buy . . . the Hawes seemed to get it right. Once again she recognized her luck, being under their wing.

'Charlie said there'd be an accident with Birdie,' she remembered.

They started back through the woods. They were at the far end now, beyond the National

Trust house, and had to take a walkers' footpath to get back to the road. Hugh led Birdie from Swallow, and she walked calmly between them.

'Whatever are you riding?' he asked.

Rowan explained. 'It won't jump even a pole on the ground.'

'Too fat,' Hugh said.

'Could you get him over a little jump?'

'Of course.'

'I bet you couldn't!' Rowan remembered the dispiriting feeling of Honeypot slowing down beneath her, in spite of her flailing legs.

'Bet you.'

'Go on, I bet you can't!' He was so conceited!

'I'll show you. What will you bet me? Your pudding at supper? It's treacle tart. I saw it this morning.'

'All right, pig. I bet you my treacle tart.'

'Let me get on him. You ride Swallow.'

Rowan blinked, not foreseeing this move, but her heart leapt with excitement. Hugh gave her a leg-up on Swallow and handed her Birdie's reins. He moved off ahead of her down a grass ride that led back to the road and Rowan followed. She felt as if she had turned into a member of the top ride, ready to ride in the team, not nervous at all. The sight of Swallow's thick blue-black mane and little ears pricked ahead of her made her shiver with joy. There was a handy log lying on the side of the path just ahead of them, about a foot high.

Hugh turned Honeypot towards it and managed to get him into a trot. Rowan thought he would jump, but at the last minute he stopped dead. Hugh sat like a rock and would not let him turn aside, pressing him on with his legs and, after a little dithering, Honeypot actually jumped – a proper jump, not a step-over.

'There.' Hugh tried not to look pleased but the thought of the treacle tart evoked a self-satisfied grin.

How was it done, Rowan wondered crossly? Roma had tried it and she had tried it, all to no avail. Hugh took Birdie's reins from her, but didn't ask to change ponies again, and when they came to another log she turned Swallow to face it and pressed him into a trot. What possessed her to do this she had no idea, only the memory of seeing him flying over the timber in the wood with Hugh leaning up on his neck and remembering her feeling of longing that it might be herself . . . and Swallow lengthened his stride and flew the log, so effortlessly that she did not budge in the saddle. True, it was only small, but Rowan felt as if she were riding for

England at Badminton. Her confidence swelled and took off like a hot air balloon, so that it was all she could do to stop belting off down the inviting path for the sheer hell of it.

'What on earth do you two think you're doing?'

An angry voice interrupted her moment of glory and she looked up to see Charlie coming down the track ahead of her, riding Out of the West. Swallow skidded to a halt and Hugh ambled up on Honeypot. To Rowan's dismay Charlie was obviously furious, and his dark blue gaze was directed straight at her.

She had no excuse at all.

'Don't lose your rag. We went to look for Birdie,' Hugh said. 'No-one else bothered.'

'Not surprising, considering what's been happening. Birdie was the least of their worries. Get off that pony, Rowan, before we have another broken neck. At once!'

His voice was icy. Rowan felt a terrible flush of shame engulfing her. She slithered off immediately, all her Badminton feeling squashed flat, and Hugh said, 'It's not her fault. I told her to swap ponies.'

'You are completely irresponsible,' Charlie snapped at him.

'Just because you're instructing the top ride

78

you needn't get so uppity. You sound like Mrs Prebble,' Hugh said, giving Honeypot back to Rowan and taking Swallow. 'What are you in such a stew about?'

'Oh, come off it, Hugh – can't you see how bad things look, without taking any more risks? Matty's really damaged herself – it's not just peanuts, and Mrs Prebble's going to blame us, I can see it coming. Everyone else has gone home and I'm sent to look for Birdie and find you two idiots playing about on your own. You know that's forbidden.'

'Why's everyone gone home? I thought your ride was going to do cross-country after us?'

'Well, the accident's cast a gloom. It all looks rather serious. Auntie M couldn't face the prospect of Prissy Hicks going cross-country on this beast on the same afternoon. She thought two in hospital on the same day might give her a bad name.'

'I thought that was what they bought her for, so that Princess Priscilla can win everything?'

'Yes, that was the idea. But this horse is far too high-powered for Prissy. She's not had much experience. Her parents are potty, getting her this.'

Hugh cast a reflective eye over the gorgeous horse. Rowan could see the way his mind was working . . . five years from now . . . 'Pity we couldn't get a horse like that in the yard.'

'We've never had that sort of money. Dad bought some good ones, but they're the ones that sold the fastest.'

For all Charlie's skill, he had never had a good horse of his own, Rowan realized. Even Bonzo's mother, Fedora, had been sold, and broken Charlie's heart for a little while. He looked splendid on Out of the West as he walked out beside them, the gleaming coat shadowed against the afternoon sun above the down. Rowan, falling behind on old Honeypot, was grateful his wrath was short-lived. She could not bear to be seen wanting by Charlie.

A gloom lay over the camp that evening. Word came from Mrs Prebble that Matty was being airlifted to Stoke Mandeville, the hospital for spinal injuries. Mrs Prebble would not be returning. This was far worse than the usual mild concussion, broken leg or collarbone, and outside the Pony Club's experience so far, although Auntie Millie knew plenty about such injuries. Her face was very stern and unhappy that night. Rowan was on washing-up duty after supper and found the atmosphere in the kitchen amongst the mothers on duty equally gloomy, all of them thinking it might have been their child.

'It's a risk every time a child mounts a pony, we all know that,' said one.

'Well, if she will buy her child such a difficult pony, what does she expect?' said Roma's mother, who did not know that Birdie had been sold to the Prebbles by Charlie Hawes, the mother of whom was drying dishes at her side.

Two other mothers, who knew the facts, exchanged worried looks at the turn the conversation had taken. Joan Hawes said nothing but her old look, which had started to dissipate over the last few days, had come back, Rowan noticed. Rowan thought of poor Roma, whom she had left weeping in the pig-trailer, being stranded in her ambition on the hopeless Honeypot who was undoubtedly safe, but so safe as to make Roma's pony life a complete waste of time.

When she went back to the pig-trailer she tried to cheer Roma up but Roma said her parents would never buy her another pony until she grew out of Honeypot. Rowan had another idea.

'Perhaps if you bring him up to High Hawes – High Horse,' she corrected herself quickly, 'they might get him to go.' She told her about Hugh making him jump the log.

Roma looked slightly more optimistic at this idea, and said she would ask her parents. Rowan thought perhaps she had got the stable a customer. When she went to the stable to see Jones was happy for the night she mentioned it to Lizzie, but Lizzie was too upset about Birdie to be much interested. She too had been crying.

'Poor Birdie, it wasn't her fault. Now everyone's saying Mrs Prebble will have her shot.'

'She wouldn't! I saw it happen – it was a complete accident!'

'You saw it?'

'Yes. I was right there. Birdie slipped up. She didn't fall on her on purpose.'

'Oh, Rowan, you must stick up for her! If you actually saw it, you're the only person who can say this.'

'And Roma. And a few of us. We all saw it.'

'Oh, good. I thought nobody saw. And Mrs Prebble is so beastly! She's been blaming Charlie for selling her the pony, and we all know at home how she insisted on having her. It will be terribly bad for setting up High Horse, if she goes round telling everyone this. And Matty in Stoke Mandeville!'

'Auntie Millie knows it's not your fault – I heard her talking to Charlie and she backed him up.'

'We'll just have to show everyone on Saturday. Shrimp and Hugh and you on Jones. How perfectly *safe* all our ponies are. You especially, Rowan, because you're a pupil, not family.'

Rowan was a bit appalled at this, but did not say so. On Saturday all the parents came for the last day and they had a big competition – show-jumping and cross-country, even for the smallest ride. She had been fairly confident about it, so obliging was dear Jones, but now the thought of such responsibility put her off, rather. Suppose she let them all down by falling off and breaking something? Apparently, in spite of the Hicks's clout, Prissy was not going to be allowed to go cross-country on Saturday. Auntie Millie had put her foot down. Prissy was saying her dad would be furious.

'We can't risk it, Priscilla.' Auntie Millie had her rat-trap expression on. 'We can't wave a magic wand in one week flat. You need long, steady training with a good instructor to get together with that young horse. I shall speak to your father. It will be me he will be angry with, so don't get upset.'

Prissy looked rather marvellous when she was angry, her chestnut mane bouncing with indignation, her amber eyes flashing like traffic lights. She turned away and went back across the yard to her loose-box. At the same moment Charlie came to fetch the old Land-Rover to drive home in, and Priscilla stopped to talk to him. Rowan came out of Jones's box in time to see Charlie put his arm round Priscilla and give her a comforting hug. Priscilla's expression changed. Instead of sending out sparks, she now looked like the cat who had found the cream. Her lovely amber eyes shone full beam on Charlie.

Rowan watched, goggle-eyed, as Charlie gave her a really soppy smile. His hand came up and caressed her hair, then he realized they were not alone and stood off, and grinned in his usual way, and Rowan heard him say, 'Don't worry. We'll sort it out with your dad. It's not your fault. You're great.'

Yuk, thought Rowan. She was furious with jealousy and stormed back across the field to the pig-trailer. How could he! *Her* Charlie! With that really revolting girl! Her day was ruined. She stomped back to the pig-trailer and Roma gave her a Mars bar.

'We've been invited to a midnight feast over the stables tonight. With your lot – Hugh and them. Hugh's pinched one of the trifles for tomorrow's dinner. It's in Swallow's stable with a bucket over it. You're not to tell anyone else though.'

Rowan forgot about Charlie for the time being.

CHAPTER FIVE

The midnight feast turned into a rather sombre discussion, not surprisingly, since the events of the day. After they had eaten the trifle they sat in a circle in the moonlight that shone through the dormer window and gossiped. (Rowan kept her revelations about Charlie and Prissy to herself.) Hugh and Lizzie and Shrimp were there, and two boys from the Red ride: Alan Finch and a weedy blond boy called Bas, and Babar had been invited. She had been having a thoroughly satisfactory week on the Armchair and was quite a changed character, Rowan thought, far more outgoing and cheerful.

''E's wonderful,' she said simply. ''E does just anything.'

'Huh,' said Roma crossly.

'It's not looks, is it?' Lizzie said. 'He doesn't look anything, and neither does Fable, but they're both lovely.'

'So's Jones,' said Rowan loyally, noticing

85

that no-one was saying how wonderful Swallow was.

'Blue-roans are horrid,' Hugh said.

'They're not!' said Shrimp. 'Roans are lovely. Pinkie's wonderful. And Jones is a dear. It's just your ponies that are horrid. Cascade and Swallow.'

'Cascade—'

'Oh, shut up,' said Lizzie. 'It's Birdie we want to talk about. What's going to happen to Birdie. We've got an idea.'

'Who's got an idea?' Shrimp asked.

'Me and Hugh, and Charlie a bit. We mentioned it to him but he's rather doubtful. It depends— '.

'Charlie said don't tell him, he'd rather not know,' Hugh said.

'Tell him what?'

'We want to ride Birdie cross-country on Saturday, just to show everybody how good she is, and safe. She could easily win the Intermediate, with a proper rider.'

'Who's we?' Babar demanded. 'You, I suppose?'

'Well, I could, but it would be better if it was Lizzie. Birdie knows Lizzie, and everyone thinks Lizzie's – well – they think she's— ' He paused.

'Not much good,' said Shrimp amiably.

Lizzie said firmly, 'If Hugh gets her round they'll just say, oh, Hugh can get anything round, but if I get her round they'll be impressed.'

'That's what I meant,' Hugh said.

Babar gave him a disgusted look and said, 'You are *pathetic*, Hugh! 'Ow about me riding 'er? – that would show 'em!'

'Or Rowan,' suggested Shrimp.

'We're serious,' said Lizzie earnestly, not put off by Hugh's insults and the others' sarcasm. 'I am sure she'll go for me and it would just show everybody that she's not a rogue. Mrs Prebble will go round telling everyone – you know she will.'

In the moonlight Lizzie's face was flushed with earnestness. Rowan knew perfectly well that when she used to ride Birdie she was nervous of her and longed for an easier pony. It was only her loyalty that was spurring her to attempt this proving of Birdie's good name. Rowan thought it was very risky, remembering Birdie's wild behaviour under Matty.

'It was only that she didn't like the way Matty rode her,' she said.

Babar looked very doubtful. 'Surely 'er bad experiences this week can't be cured overnight? You can't be sure she'll go round for you. And 'ow will you start? When they see you they'll shout and scream at you to get off.'

'Auntie Millie and Otty and them all station themselves in the wood to watch people go round. By the time I pass them they won't be able to stop me. The starter's going to be Jerry Patterson and he won't know Birdie from Fable, and the stewards at the start are all parents who don't know either. It's just a question of riding her up the lane when no one who matters is looking. To most people she looks much like Fable anyway. It's only afterwards, when we've shown them how good she is, we'll make sure everyone knows it's Birdie.'

Rowan was terribly impressed. She thought Lizzie very brave indeed. The others, she could see, were impressed too.

Hugh said, solemnly, 'It matters to the stable, to High Horse. It would be marvellous for Mum and Charlie and Josephine, if we proved to everybody that we don't sell people duds. That Birdie is as good as gold. Especially for Mum.'

'As long as she is,' Babar said.

There was a long silence. Rowan found she was getting the shivers, a sort of excitement mixed with fear, and the glory of being involved with these daring plans. It was dark in the loft save for a wide sheet of moonlight that slid in through the dormer window, and their anxious faces had a blueish cast, in keeping with the seriousness of the discussion. Below them they could hear ponies shifting, sighing, munching hay, the occasional snort.

'Suppose she isn't as good as gold?' Babar asked.

'She will be. I know she will be.' Lizzie leaned forward earnestly. 'I know her better than anyone else.' Her great mass of springy pale hair flared round her head like a ghostly halo. She was very intense and caring, not like her brash brother. 'I can't bear the thought of beastly Mrs Prebble blaming it all on her.'

'And us,' said Hugh.

'No.' Babar was thoughtful. After a long silence she said, 'I don't think you ought to let Charlie and Josephine know what you intend to do.'

'They'd agree with us!' Hugh said. 'They would want— '

'They might want, but they can't. Not now that they're instructors. Don't be stupid. They have to take the other side, being good and correct. Josephine is terribly instructorish, isn't she, Shrimp?'

'Yes. Almost as bad as Mrs Prebble. She's not a bit nicer to Babar and me in the ride.'

'Charlie's nicer to Princess Priscilla,' Alan said, and laughed.

'They were holding hands in the feed shed,' said Bas.

'What! Charlie?' Lizzie squeaked.

'He says she needs a lot of help.'

'That's true,' Rowan said staunchly. 'He says Out of the West is too strong for her.'

'Lucky for him,' Alan said with a smile.

'But she's awful!'

'Very pretty,' said Bas.

The boys started wrangling about something else and the plot for Birdie was forgotten for the time being. But every time Rowan thought about it she got the shivers again.

'I don't know how she dares,' Roma whispered when they were back in bed.

'No.'

Both Rowan and Roma knew the Hawes were made of sterner stuff than they were. Yet Rowan knew that it was much harder for Lizzie to do such a daring deed than it would have been for Hugh. When she groomed Jones beside Fable in the morning, Rowan could see that Lizzie was pale and fraught. She had asked to look after Birdie too, and had been in to feed and groom her, but Auntie Millie said no-one was to ride her.

'I said she needs exercising, but Auntie Millie said no. Absolutely not.'

'She'll be a real handful by Saturday, if she's not ridden out.'

'Hugh says we'll ride her tonight, when the night patrol's gone off. He's going to smuggle her tack out of the tack room before it's locked up and hide it in the loft, and come with me on Jerry's bicycle. You mustn't tell anyone!'

'No fear!'

'Lucky she's in the end box, on her own. We think we can get her out without anyone hearing, if we keep on the grass. Just hope none of the ponies whinny. Then I'll be able to see if she's her old self with me.'

'You are brave!'

'It matters,' Lizzie muttered fiercely. 'For our stable. Now Dad's gone.' Rowan was appalled to see tears running down Lizzie's cheeks. She did see that life was very uncertain for them since Mr Hawes had died, and tried to be as sympathetic as possible.

'If I can do anything to help— '

Lizzie said, 'Thanks. You might. I can't bank on Hugh helping tonight. You know what he's like – if the boys decide to get up to some fun he'll want to stay. So if he lets me down, you can help instead.'

Rowan nearly died of fright. When she had offered to help, she hadn't meant that! Her fingers trembled as she pulled up Jones's girths.

'I'll come for you,' Lizzie said. 'When the night patrol's finished.'

Rowan rode out feeling very anxious. Unlike Hugh, Lizzie was a worrier, and Rowan rather thought she was the same. Seeing Lizzie cry gave her a guilty qualm, for the plain fact was that she had scarcely given her deserted mother a thought during the week, so taken up was she with this amazing new life. She had no father either any more. She hadn't really taken it in yet. Her mother came to camp every day to help in the kitchen, and they had scarcely had any conversation beyond, 'Do you need a clean shirt?' and 'Can you bring me another bucket? Jones trod in it and squashed it flat.' But her mother hadn't looked particularly deserted; she had always appeared to Rowan quite cheerful.

At lunchtime that day she took the trouble to observe her mother. Unlike Joan Hawes, she looked about five years younger than she remembered, and was laughing with Roma's rather dour mother over a strange trifle that someone had brought in as a supper contribution.

Rowan said to her, 'Are you all right?' and

her mother gave her a startled look and said, 'Yes, of course.'

'About Dad – you're all alone now I'm away too.'

'Oh no, I'm staying with Joan at High Hawes. And Charlie and Josephine come back, and Jerry's there, and we have a high old time with the youngsters – all the gossip and the stories they have to tell about you children. I'm really enjoying myself.'

'But what about Dad?'

'What about him?' her mother said sharply. 'If he prefers other company, the same goes for me too.' Then, more kindly, 'Don't worry, Rowan. We'll be all right.' And she put her arm round her and gave her a hug. 'Are you missing him?'

'No. I thought you were.'

And her mother laughed.

Rowan wondered why people got married in the first place. Did it all change afterwards, from being all gooey like Charlie and Prissy, to shouting at each other like her mother and father?

'Are your parents happily married?' she asked Roma.

Roma said gloomily, 'Yes, I think so. You could fool me sometimes.'

Joan Hawes was obviously grieving over Fred:

93

it showed. Yet he had shouted quite a lot and had not been what Rowan thought of as lovable. Auntie Millie had a dear old farmer husband, always smiling. Mrs Prebble seemed to have discarded Mr Prebble, as he was never mentioned. Mr and Mrs Hicks seemed to be on speaking terms. Perhaps she was unlucky. But, curiously, like her mother, she couldn't say she was sorry her father had departed. He had been so bad-tempered, and not enthusiastic about her new-found obsession with ponies.

At the end of the afternoon Otty said to Rowan, 'On the last day, when we all go cross-country for the competition, I think it would be nice if Roma could go round on Jones. It would give her so much confidence, and he's such a genuine pony, he's bound to get her round. It means he'll have to go twice, but he's quite up to it, if you don't mind.'

'No, of course not.'

'She's so unhappy with Honeypot.'

Rowan didn't mind, but was slightly put out by the implication that Jones would go for anyone, even a duffer. She supposed it was true. No-one would have offered Roma Swallow to get round on.

When she put Jones away, Lizzie came back with Fable and said, 'I've told Hugh I'd rather go with you tonight. I don't want him letting me down at the last moment. He's like that.'

She must have noticed Rowan's face turn pale. She said, 'There's nothing to worry about. Otty's going to lunge Birdie after tea, and she's going out for a bit in the schooling meadow, until it gets dark. So she won't be too fresh.'

Rowan thought Lizzie was trying to convince herself, as much as reassure her. She felt sick when she went to bed. She told Roma what was going to happen, and set her alarm clock for three in the morning. Lizzie had said it would be going light, but Rowan was sure it wouldn't. Roma wanted to come too, but Rowan said she couldn't. 'Instead of' would have been all right, but not 'as well'.

The news had come through from Stoke Mandeville that Matty had a spinal injury and her legs were paralysed. The only good thing about it was that they didn't think it was a permanent injury. They thought she would recover, but it would take time. Mrs Prebble had rung the news through to Auntie Millie, but was staying at the hospital. Lizzie had cried again when she heard the news. Rowan knew it was for Birdie more than Matty. But the seriousness of the accident was certainly very depressing. Nobody thought that sort of thing happened to anybody like them, only to a few adults out racing and hunting. Collarbones cracked by the dozen, but that was nothing. Welfare had only had one black eye and a trodden-on big toe the whole week, and that was the usual sort of haul, not dreadful things like Matty's.

Rowan lay in the darkness wondering what would happen if Lizzie was wrong about Birdie, and Birdie tossed her off tonight, and she was left to pick up the pieces. It didn't bear thinking about! She could not sleep and was wide awake when her alarm clock went off. She squashed it immediately so that Roma wouldn't wake, and crawled out of her sleeping bag. She was already dressed and only had to pull on her anorak. She felt stiff and awful, and shivered uncontrollably as she peered out across the field. She couldn't tell if it was cold or fright. Both, probably. Her teeth chattered. The field was silent and bathed in bright moonlight, and when she set off for the yard she made a a bright trail in the dew for all the world to see. All the horse-boxes and caravans slumbered, the midnight antics long finished. Rowan longed to be back snug in her sleeping bag.

She made a detour round the back of the stables and crept in from the drive to Birdie's box, which was the nearest to the gate. She was afraid going through the yard might provoke a greedy whinny from an alert pony. They did not necessarily sleep all night, any more than their riders did. Her shivering stilled by the time she got to the loose-box and she felt slightly more optimistic, especially when she found Birdie ready saddled and bridled, and Lizzie waiting for her.

'I couldn't sleep,' Lizzie whispered. 'I came out early.'

'I couldn't either.'

'This is the worst bit, getting out.'

Birdie was nervous, excited by this strange routine, and churning about rather. They had to cross the tiled bit outside the stable before they could get on to the grass, then cross to the gateway where the scrunchy gravel took over. Lizzie had 'borrowed' the bike from Jerry in the afternoon, and it was leaning against the end of the stables.

'Keep your fingers crossed,' Lizzie whispered.

Rowan could see that she was now absorbed in the task at hand and her white fear had changed to excitement. They opened the door, lifting it so it didn't scrape, and Lizzie led Birdie out quickly towards the gate. The next-door pony put its head out and whinnied. Rowan, her bloodstream pulsing with fright, grabbed the bike and scurried out after Lizzie.

'Go back and shut the door,' Lizzie hissed. 'If anyone comes to look— '

Rowan raced back. The pony watched her expectantly, but did not whinny again. Rowan dragged the door to. Lizzie had already hopped on and was disappearing down the drive, riding on the grass verge, at a rapid trot. Rowan grabbed the bike and pedalled madly after her. She was out of breath, but the worst of the frights had receded. When they got to the road, Lizzie pulled up and waited for her. She was laughing.

'Piece of cake!'

Rowan felt slightly indignant, knowing that her part in the adventure was to sort things out in case Birdie was difficult and Lizzie got carted or thrown. It wasn't over yet. Birdie was excited, not unnaturally, at this unusual outing, and pranced about as Lizzie held her. Her hooves made a ringing clatter on the road which seemed to echo across the silent fields. It was cold and the grass was heavy with dew. The sky was clear and the enormous yellow disc of the full moon seemed to stare at them as if outraged. They were the only signs of life in the whole world. Rowan was still half a town girl, used to street lights and traffic all night, and hadn't yet become accustomed to the austere silence of the country night. She cycled along beside Birdie feeling that all her senses were on full alert, half afraid, half in wonder at the beauty of the sleeping valley whose shadows seemed to reach out to enclose them. She dared not say anything. On Lizzie's face was what she recognized as a typical Hawes expression: a glowing satisfaction at taking on something rather more than she knew she could chew. Birdie's shadow stretched across the road and up the hillside.

'What are you going to do?' Rowan asked.

'Just school around the park, go over a few jumps, that's all.'

They came to the park and Rowan opened the gate for Birdie, taking care to close it behind her – good Pony Club practice as she had been taught. Lizzie rode away and Rowan watched her. Birdie was a beautiful looking pony, nearly all thoroughbred, a bright bay with black points and a lovely fluent mover. But her thoroughbred spirit was not suited to a child rider and she quickly became excited and eager to go. Lizzie, knowing her well, kept her working calmly, trotting in large circles, stopping, turning, standing still. Only after half an hour did she put her at the fallen log, riding into it at a steady trot. Birdie jumped without hesitation, then tossed her head, wanting to go on. Lizzie brought her back to a walk and trotted some more steady circles. Again she jumped, and this time Birdie was calmer.

Lizzie brought her back to Rowan who sat shivering on one of the tree stumps.

'There. She remembers me, how we do it. According to Charlie, she never settled down with Matty at all. She'll go cross-country all right.'

They rode home slowly.

Lizzie said, hesitantly, 'I'd forgotten how lovely she is. After Fable.'

'But I thought you hated her! You said— '

'I know what I said. Yes, I love Fable because she's so easy. She never gives me frights. I'm always frightened on Birdie. She always feels as if she's going to take off. She's sort of super – super-charged. When we used to ride out on the downs I was always a bit frightened. Now, with Fable, it's fun.'

'What about Saturday then? Doing cross-country – will you be frightened?'

'Yes,' said Lizzie. 'I shall be terrified.'

'You haven't got to do it!'

'Yes. Yes, I have.'

Rowan tried to digest all these difficult pronouncements but was beginning to feel rather tired, not to say frozen. Birdie jigged about rather, but Rowan kept out of her way and cycled ahead of her up the drive to the stable yard. She propped the bike up against the wall and went to open the stable door. Birdie came in through the gate and as her hooves clattered momentarily on the tiles her neighbour stuck his head out over his door and let out a loud welcoming whinny. Birdie threw up her head and neighed back. Fable, hearing her from the other side of the yard, threw her head over the door and called a greeting, followed by Jones and Swallow. The night was suddenly rent by jolly equine conversation.

'Oh, lor', someone'll come looking! Hark at them!' Lizzie hissed.

She dragged Birdie through the door. 'Shut it!' she said to Rowan. 'Quick, take off her bridle!'

She undid the girths while Rowan fumbled with the bridle. They pulled off the tack and Lizzie threw it in the corner and covered it with straw. Then she grabbed a handful of straw and furiously rubbed the saddle marks off Birdie's back. Birdie put her head out of the door and whinnied some more and then, always a greedy pony, turned to attack her haynet.

Lizzie looked out over the door to see if anything was happening and shot back immediately.

'Someone's coming. I saw a torch! Jeez, what shall we do?' Then, taking a hold of her panic: 'They might not come right down here. We must sit tight.'

'Where?' Rowan squeaked.

'Here!'

Lizzie grabbed her and sat down on the floor hard against the wall beside the door. They pulled some straw over their legs but there wasn't enough spare to cover them. Even some of the tack showed, they noticed, but it was too late to do anything about that.

'What'll happen if they see us?'

'We'll be sent home in disgrace.'

Sent home! Rowan wanted to weep. She could not imagine a worse fate – and her mother so happy making dinners, and she with all the competitions to ride in on Saturday . . . perhaps, if she was terribly lucky, a rosette to be won . . . all her dreams would be shattered. Just because she was nobly helping out instead of beastly Hugh. She *hated* Hugh!

A voice called out imperiously from the top of the yard, 'Anyone there?'

The flash of the torch made wavering beams outside the door as it travelled round the yard.

'It's Otty,' Lizzie whispered.

Rowan felt a flicker of relief – not Auntie

Millie herself. Otty slept in a caravan near the gate. It was her job to see to disturbances in the night, pony scuffles and the odd kick and one mild attack of colic so far. Nobody had thought of people disturbances. Otty's voice sounded slightly uncertain. Perhaps she was as frightened as they were?

But Otty was made of stern stuff and came boldly down the yard shining her torch into every box. They could hear her murmuring to the disturbed ponies, her voice coming nearer and nearer.

Rowan could feel her heart pounding; almost wanted to shush it to be quiet. The palms of her hands felt sweaty and she felt sick. Birdie snatched at her hay as if she had been away for a week.

'It was you making that row, wasn't it?' Otty stopped at the next-door box. 'What set you off, you old idiot?'

There was a long silence while the old idiot regarded Otty in the torchlight with innocent eyes. Lizzie and Rowan crouched lower, holding their breath.

The torch beam sprang in through the door. Birdie jerked her head up and stood looking, a mouthful of half-snatched hay dropping from her jaws. The torch took in her head and travelled down her back and dropped to her legs. Rowan saw the glint of a stirrup under the manger.

'You look warm,' Otty remarked curiously.

But Birdie, as if in league with Lizzie and Rowan, turned back to her hay to show her unconcern. She did not come nuzzling up to the two girls who crouched in agony below the half-door.

Otty turned away, and fell over the bike.

'What on earth—?'

They heard her swear and the bike crash down. The torch light jumped about.

'God Almighty, that hurt!' Otty kicked the bike.

Would it occur to her that the bike was not usually there? There was a long, long silence outside. The two girls crouched together, holding their breath. What was she doing?

Rowan thought she would burst. Then they heard a bit more swearing, and Otty's head went past the door, making back for her caravan. They waited ages longer, but the terrible frights were over and now they were exploding with giggles, which had to be muffled. They sorted out the tack and Lizzie said she would take it back to the loft with her. Rowan had to walk out across the field. Otty would be lying awake, or perhaps had her eye open still for a possible intruder.

'I'll go down the drive and come in round the back, behind the hedge,' Rowan decided.

What a night of frights! When Rowan at last got snuggled down again into her sleeping bag it was going light and nearly time to get up.

CHAPTER SIX

Rowan woke up feeling a hundred years old. She knew it was no ordinary day and only rather slowly remembered why. She was going to ride Jones in competition and had to display her talent as a product of the High Horse School of Equitation. Everyone would be watching. And Lizzie was going to ride Birdie cross-country . . . Rowan felt sick again, as well as a hundred years old. As she had only had about two hours of sleep she supposed she had good reason.

Seeing the carefree Hugh at breakfast incensed her. He had nothing to worry about at all since Swallow had proved during the week that he was a winner (which of course Rowan had known all along) and Hugh expected to win his usual number of cups and rosettes, just as if he had been riding Cascade. He knew the practice with Birdie had been successful, and saw no reason why Lizzie should be in a stew about her afternoon's prospect and certainly did not expect her to beat him. Rowan could see that Lizzie was, in fact, very frightened, more of the trouble she would get into afterwards than of the ride itself. But when Rowan tried to suggest it might be wiser not to do it, she said defiantly, 'I've got to. It's to prove to everyone we don't sell duds.'

It was true, Rowan noticed, as the parents started to arrive to help arrange the course, that there was a lot of gossip going around about the accident and the reasons for it. Quite naturally it was the great talking point. Rowan heard someone say, 'They bought the pony off the Hawes – makes you wonder a bit, doesn't it? They must have known.'

She tried not to think about it, knowing that if she was in a dreadful nervous stew Jones might get worried too. It was a beautiful day and there was a terrific lot to do, and she wasn't the only one in a panic about not making a fool of herself in the afternoon.

Another crisis was looming in the Princess Priscilla department, as apparently Auntie Millie had forbidden her to take Out of the West cross-country.

'My parents will be furious!' Prissy wailed.

'Send them to me. I will explain,' Auntie

Millie barked. 'A week is not long enough to work miracles.'

This remark upset Priscilla. She sobbed to Charlie, 'Why is it a miracle for me to ride Out of the West cross-country?'

Hugh reported that Charlie went all sloppy and told her she was marvellous but the horse just needed more schooling, instead of saying (according to Hugh), 'Your parents were mad to buy you such a high-powered horse when you're a right dozy rider who couldn't get round on Jones, let alone Out of the West.'

Rowan was riled that her pony was used by everyone as the one *anyone* could ride. But Prissy and her parents bought mounts for looks, for vanity. Dear Babar, Rowan was heartened to see, was all smiles to be riding the Armchair, who was just as ugly in his way as her own Black Diamond, whom everyone had laughed at for years. With his too-large blaze and carthorse legs, he had a heart of gold.

Mr and Mrs Hicks arrived at lunchtime in their Mercedes and parked conspicuously alongside the vast horse-box that Prissy had lived in all the week. They joined her inside for their gin and tonics, and Mr Hicks emerged ten minutes later with a face like thunder, demanding to talk to Mrs Mildmay. Everyone pretended to go about their business but managed to get close enough to overhear the exchange.

'What's this ridiculous instruction about my girl not riding in the competition this afternoon?'

'I don't want another accident, Mr Hicks. Priscilla is not yet experienced enough to take such a difficult horse cross-country.'

Mr Hicks turned from red to purple.

'Priscilla is perfectly capable! That horse is a trained and schooled jumper. We had it from the best hands. We were only interested in the best, and that's what we bought. I dispute your opinion.'

'Yes, well, you may. But I run this camp and my word here goes.'

'You told me a week at camp would work wonders with the horse. You led me to believe— '

'It has worked wonders, but more work has to be done, Mr Hicks.' Auntie Millie's jaw was sticking out like Land's End. 'Priscilla's instructor speaks very highly of her progress. But more time is needed.'

'I would like to speak to her instructor!'

'By all means. Go and find Charlie,' Auntie Millie snapped at Hugh, who was goggling nearby. 'Tell him Mr Hicks wants a word.'

She turned back to Mr Hicks and said scathingly, 'This is the Pony Club, Mr Hicks. Not Gleneagles. Perhaps Priscilla has grown out of it.'

Rowan felt herself getting steamed up at the thought of poor Charlie facing this irascible man. She heard Otty say, 'I thought it was supposed to be a fun day,' sadly, and Auntie Millie said to her, 'We've got Lucy Prebble gracing us with her presence this afternoon as well. This is just the start.'

Mrs Prebble! Of all the people likely to torpedo Lizzie's attempt to ride Birdie Mrs Prebble herself was the most likely. With luck she would be given a job far away from the start of the cross-country. She must!

Charlie ambled up, fortunately dressed in his instructor's best, with a tie and his boots shining, and said, 'You want me?'

Mr Hicks looked him up and down as if he were a yearling at the sales and said cuttingly, 'How old are you?'

'Twenty-five,' Charlie said.

Mr Hicks didn't know how to answer this, obviously not believing him, but not actually brave enough to accuse him of lying.

'I understand you've been teaching my daughter all the week?'

'Yes, sir.'

'And what's this nonsense about her not being allowed to go cross-country?'

Charlie shot a hopeful glance at Auntie Millie for help but Auntie Millie was glaring unhelpfully into the middle distance.

'It would be wiser to give it a miss. She hasn't had enough time yet, to get used to the horse.'

'She's no good, you're saying?'

'No. She's very good. But the horse gets rather steamed up. He's likely to take off with her. And that wouldn't be very useful.'

'I want to see my horse perform, that's what I'm here for. If you're such a fine instructor I suggest you take him round.' He spoke in a sarcastic tone of voice that clearly implied he thought the challenge would be refused. But Charlie immediately said, 'Certainly. I'd like to.'

Auntie Millie opened her mouth, then shut it again. Mr Hicks stormed off to make trouble somewhere else and Auntie Millie said to Charlie, 'Was that wise?'

'No. It's a bit stupid really.'

They looked at each other and grinned. Auntie Millie shrugged and laughed. 'That's my boy.'

Otty, taking all this in, shook her head in despair.

'They're all batty in this Pony Club,' she said. 'All of them.'

Rowan thought she didn't know the half of it yet.

She groomed Jones until he gleamed dark bluey-grey like a suit of armour and then went to lunch with a white-faced Lizzie and a gloomy Roma. Hugh and Babar looked happy enough, Hugh because he knew he was going to win everything and Babar because, for once, she knew her pony would jump when asked, not spectacularly, but with an amiable heave that generally left the obstacle in one piece. Lizzie had to go away and be sick in the loo.

Rowan and Roma were to do their cross-country first, being in the junior group. Shrimp, Babar, Lizzie and Hugh were all in the Intermediate, but only Hugh was expected to do any good. Lizzie's Fable, whom everyone thought she was going to ride, was too slow to win and sometimes stopped; the same applied to the Armchair, and Shrimp had found Pinkie had a mind of her own and hated leaving Bonzo behind, having become attached to him like a real mother. Hugh said she should go cross-country with Bonzo running behind, and Shrimp actually asked Auntie Millie if she could but received a not unexpected refusal. She was determined to prove to Auntie Millie that she was not just a pretty show rider with red hair ribbons. Her hair was now severely secured with brown rubber bands. She was preoccupied with her problems, which loomed to her as large as Lizzie's. Pauline Watkins came up to them as they finished their lunch and said, 'Why do you all look so miserable?'

Nobody replied.

She said, 'I suppose because it's all going to finish this afternoon.'

The others went back to the stables but Rowan ran after her mother and asked her what she was going to do during the afternoon.

'They tell me I've got to fence-judge. I've no idea what it entails. I'm hoping someone will tell me before the off.'

'What's Mrs Prebble doing? Is she fence-judging?'

'Yes, I think she is.'

As long as she was well stuck in the wood all would be well, but if she was anywhere near the start, Lizzie's ride was doomed. As it was, whatever happened, she would recognize Birdie and make a great fuss. Rowan's gloom deepened, and she wished heartily that Lizzie had not set her heart on this noble action for the stable. She was going to get little thanks.

Being in the lowest cross-country ride she was one of the first to go. As Jones was going twice, Rowan was going to go first and Roma last in their group, to give him plenty of time for a breather. Rowan had had strict instructions to go straight back after she had ridden and help them with the Birdie plan, and the Birdie plan was so much more difficult than riding Jones over the course that she found she was through the start almost without noticing it.

Her mother was fence-judging at the first obstacle, an easy row of straw bales, and Rowan saw her excited face as Jones whizzed over. Lizzie had told her to find out where Mrs Prebble was fence-judging, but Rowan suddenly found that Jones was far more of a handful on his own than when they had practised the course all together and rather forgot about everything else. Her seat was still very insecure and she wasn't too proud to take a large handful of mane at each approach. 'Much better than hanging on by the reins,' sensible Otty had told her. She was going quite a lot faster than she had meant to, but it was rather exciting. Her course was only very low, with scrambles over banks and through ditches, and it was more a matter of steering accurately than anything else. It sometimes crossed the Intermediate course which was much more respectable, and the last bit came back into the park alongside some horrific jumps for the Seniors which were left over from a proper One Day Event. Otty had told them that one day they would sail over these and enjoy every minute of it. Who on? was the question. Hugh said Swallow would fly them and thought he ought to ride in the Senior group, but he had been squashed. For a moment, coming home, Rowan felt a surge of confidence that made her feel that Jones too would fly them if she faced him in the right direction. He was such an honest pony, and she hadn't disgraced herself as she had feared, but was jumping into the park with her feet still in the stirrups and her reins nicely arranged, not out like the washing, and was even able to pull up, unlike some who were apt to disappear from sight into the hinterland of the National Trust gardens.

'Well done!' shouted Jerry Patterson, who was time-keeping (no doubt pleased that the pony he had recommended hadn't blotted his copybook).

Her mother was making excited, arm-waving gestures from her place by the hay-bales and in her excitement missed out the next competitor (which was later to cause confusion in the scoring caravan).

Rowan realized she had never looked for Mrs Prebble. But she was so excited by her successful round that it was hard to feel bad about it. If she never saw her, with luck she wasn't there at all. She couldn't help bubbling over with pride – a clear round! – even if it was potty stuff . . . she hadn't fallen off. She was a credit to the High Horse School of Equitation! Even Hugh would be pleased with her. But her duty was back at Lizzie's side. She handed Jones over to Roma, who said she would ride him round quietly, and got on to fat Honeypot who was only too pleased to be headed back to the stables and waddled along keenly. Several riders were going up to the course and asked her how she had gone on, and it was sweet to smile and shout, 'Clear!' They shouted back, 'Well done!' and the whole Pony Club thing seemed suddenly a very good idea. If it wasn't for the Birdie thing, this last day would be absolute bliss.

People were charging about all over the place, some going out to show-jump in the field, the little ones gymkhana-ing, cross-country competitors coming and going down the lane. In the confusion it was easy to tack up Birdie in her box. There were no instructors around; they were all out organizing things, and the yard was relatively peaceful. Roma had had strict instructions to hurry back after her round so that they would know when the Intermediate was due to start. The Green ride was to jump first – that included Shrimp and Babar, then the Red ride which was Hugh and Lizzie. Shrimp and Babar said they would stay down there in case they could be useful. Lizzie was down to jump second in her section after a girl called Anna Bambridge on a bay cob, and Hugh followed her on Swallow. In spite of all the tension, Rowan's good feeling after her successful round stayed with her, and she found she could be quite helpful calming Lizzie, because she felt so good herself. Roma came back on Jones grinning all over her face saying how wonderful he was, and Rowan exchanged him for Honeypot and they all rode off down the drive in a group, with Birdie in the middle.

'I'll ride Birdie in the National Trust woods until it's my turn,' Lizzie said. 'No-one will see us there.'

It all seemed more optimistic now they were under way. They got down to the park without anyone noticing Birdie, and Lizzie rode on into the woods. Birdie was very much on her toes, sensing all the excitement, but Lizzie was now calm and stern, not shivery any more.

There were two riders to go before Shrimp.

Pinkie, having left Bonzo behind, was being cantankerous and Hugh said he betted she wouldn't start.

'She will,' Shrimp said.

She was white and her jaw was stuck out like Auntie Millie's. She took Pinkie down to the start and made her trot in circles, and Pinkie kept pulling out towards the gate.

'She'll never make her,' Hugh said. 'She should've brought Cascade.'

'I could give her a lead,' Babar said. 'She'd follow Armchair.'

'She'd be disqualified.'

At this moment Auntie Millie's Land-Rover came bouncing into the field and she pulled up near Jerry.

'That's torn it,' said Hugh.

Auntie Millie got out, and plonked down on her shooting stick, chatting to Jerry. Shrimp was given the nod to start. Jerry clicked his stop-watch and Mrs Mildmay's gimlet eyes followed Pinkie's bucketing canter down to the first jump, where she stopped dead.

'Told you so,' said Hugh.

Shrimp did not turn away from the jump, but sat in the saddle and kicked Pinkie into it. Pinkie tried to swing away but Shrimp wouldn't let her, legs and heels drumming to stop her.

For such a small figure her determination against the stubborn pony was formidable. It was only when Pinkie took a step backwards that Shrimp swung her round to present her for a second time, because she knew that a step backwards counted as a refusal. (Whether Rowan's mother, the fence-judge, knew this was doubtful.) She did not take her far back, and rode at the innocuous jump again with legs flailing. Three strides away she landed Pinkie a terrific clout with her whip behind the saddle, and Pinkie shot over as if the jump were Becher's Brook itself, and Shrimp did not get left behind or even dislodged, but landed beautifully poised to drive Pinkie on into the wood.

Hugh and Babar cheered madly, and Auntie Millie was heard to shout, 'Well done.'

'She'll get round now,' Hugh said. 'But one refusal – she won't win.'

'It was good though,' Babar said. 'I couldn't 'ave done that.'

When it was her turn she rode off at her rocking-horse canter on the trusty Armchair and proceeded to do a steady clear round.

'Too slow,' said Hugh.

'I thought we wanted good advertisements,' Rowan said. 'That was a very good advertisement.'

Babar came back beaming. Rowan knew the feeling. There was nothing like it. After Babar there were only three more in her class to go, then it was the next section and Lizzie was second to go. Shrimp had spotted Mrs Prebble in the wood at the well-named coffin jump, and Auntie Millie seemed to have settled herself permanently at the start, which was not at all convenient. Hugh decided to go down and distract her when it was Lizzie's turn to go. Lizzie was keeping a watch-out and when Anna Bambridge started she emerged from her hiding-place.

Jerry Patterson, looking at his clipboard, said to Hugh, 'Your sister's next to go. Where is she?'

Hugh nodded towards the bay in the distance and said, 'She's coming.'

Jerry bawled in Lizzie's direction, 'Number thirty-three next!' Then he turned to Hugh and said, 'What's she riding? Looks like the Prebble beast.'

His voice was loud and clear but Auntie Millie was at that moment, by a stroke of magical luck, trying to make her walkie-talkie work, which was always a great effort for her. She was clicking away and talking very loudly into the microphone. Hugh rode up to Jerry and hissed, 'Don't say anything, *please*! It's for Mum, and Charlie – you haven't *noticed*!'

Jerry looked astonished, as well he might. The insouciant Hugh was the last character to look so fraught: that in itself was a shock. Perhaps Jerry thought Charlie was in on the venture, for he didn't say any more but merely looked very worried. He kept his head down, examining his stop-watch. Hugh rode boldly across to Auntie Millie and sat where she had to turn her back to the course to speak to him, and started on a long ramble about when they cleared up could they leave their stuff in the hay-loft until tomorrow because they had to ride home because Charlie was transporting somebody else in their horsebox, for money, which they needed . . . etc. etc. Swallow was very excited, sensing that he was about to go cross-country, and Auntie Millie had to jump off her shooting stick at one point to save her skin, after which she said rather tersely, 'Of course, Hugh. Do stop fussing. It's not like you. And take that dangerous pony out of my way before you do me a damage. Are you next to go?'

'Yes,' said Hugh, because Lizzie had taken her opportunity and sped through the start the minute Jerry had clicked his stop-watch for Anna's finish.

Jerry said blandly, 'Lizzie Hawes on Fable. Hugh next.'

It all happened so smoothly and so fast that Rowan and Babar and Shrimp could not believe Lizzie's luck. Birdie sped down to the straw bales and flew them in her stride before Pauline Watkins could catch her number. (Fence-judging was much harder than making sandwiches, she was thinking; she would make sure she didn't get this job again.) 'Who was that?' she shouted to the fence-judge who guarded the jump into the wood and he shouted back, 'Thirty-three! Lizzie Hawes on Fable.'

Birdie was excited but Rowan could see that Lizzie was so hyped up to do well that – like Shrimp earlier – she was riding out of her skin. When it *mattered* . . . Getting started was the hardest – whatever happened next would be an anti-climax. The deed was done. Unless Lizzie hit a tree or had an accident . . . Rowan realized she was trembling all over. She looked at Shrimp and noticed she was white as a sheet, staring towards the wood, and Babar was silent, sitting motionless on the Armchair. Only Hugh was not concerned with Lizzie, his hands entirely full with a super-charged Swallow, who was tearing long strips of grass up with his eager plunges, frantic to go. Rowan gulped, thinking of herself in Hugh's place, where she always thought she most wanted to be. Did she? Swallow was daunting. Even Hugh, the brilliant, conceited, best rider in the world, was looking worried.

In fact, so disturbed was Auntie Millie about Swallow's behaviour that she got off her shooting stick and closed it with a snap and got back into her Land-Rover. Out of the window she shouted at Hugh, 'I hope you know what you're doing, young man! I shall have a word with Josephine about that animal.' And while Hugh was taking her attention, Lizzie cantered back through the finish on Birdie, and Mrs Mildmay was back to stabbing buttons on her walkie-talkie set and shouting, 'Over to you! Roger!' and did not even see her.

Lizzie trotted back to the others and almost fell off in her relief and delight.

'She was brilliant. Clear! She didn't put a foot wrong! She was wonderful!'

She was so excited she burst into tears. They none of them watched Hugh depart, but gathered round Lizzie all with the same flooding feeling of incredible relief that the plan had been carried out so successfully. In fact, now it was over, and had been so easy, they started to wonder about why they had all been so worried.

'She went so well! No hesitation at all! She loved it!'

'Auntie Millie never even noticed!'

'But what if you've won,' said Shrimp, 'and when they give out the results they say Fable, instead of Birdie? They've got to know, else there was no point doing it.'

'That's true. You've got to tell 'um,' Babar said.

'Go and tell Jerry,' Shrimp suggested. 'Then he can tell Auntie Millie.'

'Ride over there and just see what happens,' Rowan suggested.

Lizzie was on such a high that she was no longer worried about the prospective row. She gathered herself together and started to ride back to the start. As she did so, there was a startled shout from the the fence-judge at the last fence out of the wood.

'Loose horse! Loose horse!'

'It's Swallow!' shrieked Shrimp.

Riderless, the bay pony came belting back up the field towards his friends, reins and stirrups flying. He pulled up wildly, his nostrils wide and red like a Derby winner's, sweat streaking his dark flanks. Babar nudged her pony across to cut him off and called out, 'Steady, boy! Steady on, Swallow, there's a good fellow!' He twirled around once or twice, but Babar managed to grab his reins and hang on. A fence-judge was yelling from the edge of the wood, 'Ambulance! Ambulance! Stop the next rider!' and Auntie Millie, just as Lizzie approached her on Birdie, started her engine and drove away towards the gate that led into the wood.

Rowan found it all rather hard to believe. Nothing was working out as planned. *Hugh* had fallen off! She didn't realize it was possible. Lizzie had done an exemplary clear round on Birdie and hadn't even been noticed. The ambulance people, parked on the edge of the wood eating their sandwiches, couldn't get their engine to start. Rowan watched it all going on like a spectator at a film. Lizzie, unable to catch Auntie Millie, was talking earnestly to Jerry, so at least someone would know how clever Birdie had been. The ambulance got started just as Hugh appeared, climbing over the last fence looking noticeably furious but unbloodied. Behind him, panting, came Mrs Prebble, also noticeably furious.

Babar gave Swallow's reins to Shrimp and said to Rowan, 'I'm going back to the stables. Coming?'

'Yes,' said Rowan. And they rode off together.

CHAPTER SEVEN

It was quite late in the evening when they all rode back together over the downs to High Hawes. Bonzo ran behind bucking and kicking, relieved to be free after his week of confinement. All the ponies, even Swallow, went rather wearily, but the mood was one of satisfaction, and the late, golden light still flooding over the open grass sent their shadows in long, bobbing patterns behind them as they breasted the long hill. The eternal breeze up there lifted the ponies' manes off their sweaty necks and cooled the riders' hot and dirty faces, and the skylarks sang as if the day would last forever.

'I shall remember this, always,' Rowan thought, again deeply aware of the pleasure that had come into her life with the High Hawes ponies. There were all sorts of problems ahead for all of them, but just now none of it mattered, the small successes of the day – the week – more important and more rewarding than anything that might counter them. It was far, far from Olympic gold, but the rosette that fluttered on Jones's browband meant more to Rowan, and always would, than any more illustrious ones that might come later. It was only a second, as one beastly girl had gone faster than Jones, but Rowan could not keep her eyes off the bright ribbon nestling in his thick mane. He should have worn another one, as he had gone third for Roma, but Roma had kept it. It was her first ever too. Her delirious joy had rather impressed her gloomy parents and her father had half-promised to bring Honeypot over to High Hawes for 'a bit of schooling'. ('Starving is what he'll get', Charlie had remarked, 'before anything else.')

Birdie's silver cup and rosette, for the Overall Intermediate winner, had been appropriated by the incensed Mrs Prebble. She had rattled Birdie away in her trailer at angry speed, promising that they would all hear more from her 'very shortly'.

'More what?' said Charlie afterwards. 'Lizzie showed everybody Birdie is a really good pony.'

Lizzie was the heroine. Mrs Mildmay, presenting her with the cup, made the most tactful speech of her career, managing to infer what a brilliant pony Birdie was and declaiming how

127

everyone at camp wished Matty Prebble a speedy return to health and action. She phrased it so cleverly that it made it seem that the applause and cheering that followed was all for Matty, so Mrs Prebble was overwhelmed with people's general niceness and unable to utter. It was only later that her habitual resentment returned.

Roma remarked, 'Matty might be quite nice underneath if she didn't have her for a mother.'

'Perhaps we ought to visit her in hospital,' Lizzie said. 'It must be terribly boring lying there. The summer holidays too.'

They vaguely decided that they would.

Mrs Mildmay had given Lizzie a real piece of her mind after she had realized what she had done, but Lizzie said, even though she was foul, you somehow knew that it was more for the sake of form, and underneath she thought it was great. 'Her eyes weren't cross,' Lizzie said. And afterwards, after the scorching words, she had put her arm round Lizzie's shoulder and given her a sharp hug, before walking away very quickly.

'People say she was really wild in her youth. Dad used to tell stories about her,' Hugh said.

He hadn't lost his conceit for very long, although he couldn't bear to recall the humiliation of watching everyone else taking his glory, of not being called up to receive a single rosette. Not even a white for Effort, like the dunces. It had never happened before.

'So how come the brilliant Hugh Hawes *fell off*?' his friend Alan Finch had asked derisively. 'Only lesser mortals *fall off*.'

By the time Hugh had sorted out his tale, it was one of high endeavour over impossible odds. 'Swallow bolted down the ride and some idiot of a fence-judge came out waving her arms like a lollipop lady and Swallow shied like an idiot into the trees and I got wiped off by an overhanging branch. Somebody caught him and brought him back and I knew I'd lost my chance so I decided to come back and do some of the senior jumps. I did two – he really flew over them – but over the third my stirrup leather broke and he did a colossal buck on landing and I flew off.'

Rowan had surreptitiously looked at his stirrup leather and it didn't look very broken to her, but she didn't say anything. Hugh had convinced himself quite quickly that he should have won. It was only other people's stupidity that had prevented it. Charlie, hearing this story, had just smiled.

Even Shrimp had come away happy because Pinkie had got a fourth with only one refusal and Mrs Mildmay, when she presented the rosette, whispered to her, 'I take it all back. You're not just a pretty show-girl. You're a damned good rider.'

Shrimp, even at her tender age, sensed that there was no way to explain to such as Mrs Mildmay that it wasn't just peanuts riding a show-pony to win a cup, so she sensibly smirked and said nothing. But the rosette meant a lot to her, more than the many championship ribbons she had been in the habit of tossing nonchalantly to her owners in the past.

By the time they had got home and dried off the ponies' tack marks and turned them out in the field it was almost dark. Rowan hung over the gate after the others had gone in and watched Swallow rolling down in the wet patch by the stream. Jones went down to join him, and when he had got up and shaken himself with a blubbery noise like a wet dog he stood head to tail with Jones and they started scratching each other's necks with their teeth. After Hugh's failure, Rowan knew she would never ride Swallow, yet her ambition did not waver. Her dogged devotion to 'her' pony had never faltered. In the dusk he gleamed with wellbeing, and his fatal exuberance, even in repose, was evident in the proud way he stood and the impatient way he switched his tail at the midges. The sweet sour smell of the evening grass, already wet with dew, freshly trampled by the ponies, hung in the air. Rowan stayed there, until the ponies had all separated and started to graze hungrily, and the sky had turned a deep, brilliant blue, with just a few lights showing below in the village. She shivered. She wanted to cry, for no reason. Yet she was so happy. And afraid. And, she realized suddenly, incredibly tired. She couldn't take any more in.

Her mother took her home in the car and she slept until midday the next day. When she awoke she could not believe the time. When she got downstairs her mother was just putting out lunch.

'Joan Hawes warned me,' she laughed. 'She said it takes a week to recover. I must say, I didn't wake up till almost ten myself. It's rather blissful to think there's nothing to do today.'

Life without camp did suddenly seem strange. As if one had been there for ever.

'It certainly took my mind off things,' Mrs Watkins said thoughtfully. 'It made me think what a lot of time I've been wasting all these years, just dusting and cooking and ironing your father's shirts. Going to the hairdresser.'

She certainly didn't look as if she had been to the hairdresser recently. Her blonde hair was rather scraped back and unkempt and her face was brown and her nose was peeling. But she looked fit and well and didn't have the worry lines that had habitually marked her forehead. Rowan didn't like to remark on it.

'Joan was talking about going into cooking – professionally. To make some money. Cook for dinner parties, or do wedding cakes, or sandwiches for businessmen or something. She asked if I was interested, to set something up.'

She seemed to be asking for Rowan's opinion, although not directly. But Rowan noticed her new lively expression, and recognized the importance of this almost casual remark.

'You're a real wow at icing cakes – all that wedding stuff, roses and things. I bet Mrs Hawes can't do that.'

'I love doing that sort of thing.' Her voice was wistful.

'Why don't you, then? I think it's a great idea, if you get on with Mrs Hawes so well. Do you?'

'Yes. We're not a bit alike, but we seem to get on. I think she thinks I'm rather frivolous. I've really enjoyed this last week, meeting all those people. I shall miss it now.'

They neither of them mentioned the missing Mr Watkins. Rowan found she really did not want to think about him. If he preferred somebody else to them, and cared so little that he just left them, without compunction, it hurt in a way that was very disturbing. Her *father*! Don't think about it.

'Yes. I think it would be great if you worked with Mrs Hawes.'

'I do admire her courage. It's quite dreadful, her loss. Not like mine at all. And the worry of the business and all those children. I've really had my eyes opened this week, seeing such a different sort of life – all those horsey people and farmers' wives – they're all so – so – tough. So busy all the time.'

Rowan looked round the tidy, sterile room that was their dining annexe, with her father's row of model cars on the top of a bookcase filled with Reader's Digest volumes and a picture of a vase of flowers over the mantelpiece whose fireplace was filled with an electric fire pretending to be a real one, and realized how unlike it was to any room in the Hawes' house, or Babar's or Jerry Patterson's. It didn't speak of any interest in life, beyond conformity. She wondered what Mrs Mildmay's house was like. It was said to be full of cobwebs, vast silver cups, ancient sofas and pictures of her grandfather's hunters and steeplechase winners. Hugh said it had mice.

You could hear them scuttering about. Hugh had a mouse in his bedroom but wouldn't let his mother put a trap down. He said he liked it. Mr Watkins would have died if he thought there was a mouse in his bedroom.

Mrs Watkins had gone into a sort of trance, eating her salad and thinking about the horsey women she had discovered, and Rowan, after offering her a few more words of encouragement, got on her bike and cycled up to High Hawes. She had to work very hard up there, to earn riding lessons. At the back of her mind she had decided to ask Josephine to teach her rather than Charlie. It was so important to her that she learned quickly, and being with Charlie was a distraction because she wanted him to think well of her all the time. It meant not making a fool of herself in front of him and sometimes, when you were learning, you had to risk making a fool of yourself. She thought she would concentrate more with Josephine.

★　　　★　　　★

When she arrived at High Hawes there was a large Audi in the front yard. For a moment Rowan thought it was Mr Hicks and her heart sank. Charlie had ridden Out of the West clear in the Senior cross-country and done the fastest clear round by miles, but as an instructor had ridden *hors de combat*, which meant, Rowan had discovered, not eligible for a prize. The fence-judges had been heard disputing as to whether he was in control or not – the general opinion was presumably, as he hadn't hit a tree, that he was, but he had gone past so fast most of them never got his number. Otty had also gone well on her youngster Hadrian. But Priscilla had won no rosettes and Mr Hicks had not been a happy man. Lizzie and Hugh were slumped out in the hay barn, doing nothing.

'Don't say you've come up to ride!' Hugh exclaimed in disbelief.

'I've come to work. Whose car is that?'

'It's Uncle Trevor. He says he's been trying to get Mum all week. He's got a buyer for High Hawes.'

'What!' Rowan was shocked. 'But you're not— '

'No, *we're* not,' Lizzie said. 'But the others— ' She shrugged and made a face. 'It's all doom and disaster in there this morning. That's why we've got out.'

Rowan was appalled. She could not believe anything so bad could happen to her, that her paradise could disappear! Uncle Trevor was the deceased Fred Hawes' brother, and after the funeral he had come up with this idea that High Hawes should be sold. He said the family could never make a living out of the place without Fred. Joan Hawes had disagreed and said they would run the place as a riding school, and Josephine and Charlie would teach, and buy and sell ponies. They all hated Uncle Trevor, a large bullying man, a successful butcher with a string of shops. He had offered to buy High Hawes himself to use as a fattening farm.

'I thought – I thought you had all told him – you were going to run the place between you— '

'We did,' Lizzie said. 'But you know what he's like. He's a bully. The trouble is— ' Her face was white and miserable. Even the ebullient Hugh was, for once, squashed and quiet.

Hugh said, 'He rang up last night, quite late, and said he was coming over. The timing was bad, because Josephine and Charlie had spent the whole evening saying they weren't cut out to be teachers. They hated the week at camp – the teaching part, at any rate.'

'But— '

'They enjoyed being there and that – they just don't like actually teaching,' Lizzie said. 'Charlie says he doesn't know how to put it into words, and Josephine says it just makes her cross. Of course, they've never learnt how to teach. It's something you have to learn. Just because you can do it yourself— '

'They don't want to learn anyway,' Hugh said gloomily. 'And if you want a proper riding school you have to have letters after your name. Qualifications.'

Both Mrs Prebble and Mr Hicks, Rowan remembered, had remarked on Charlie not being qualified.

'Charlie'll never get qualified,' Lizzie said. 'He can't spell.'

'He can't write,' Hugh said.

Rowan thought they must be exaggerating. 'Josephine could.'

'Not if she doesn't want to,' Lizzie said.

'But you can't sell up and go away!' Rowan wailed.

'That's what we said, and Ma told us to go away and get lost. They'll all in there yakking away, all very bad-tempered.'

'But Mum said your mother was thinking about setting up a food business – for dinner parties and weddings and things – and my mum was talking about going in with her— '

'Yeah, well, they can still do that. You don't need fifty acres and two stable yards to make sandwiches. That's what Uncle Trevor is after, the land and the stabling.'

'And the house, he said. He said we can get a house in the village.'

'But where will the horses go?'

'We sell them, daftie. What do you think?' Hugh snapped out.

Rowan could see that Hugh was as upset as she was herself. She could not believe, after such a wonderful day yesterday and all their successes, that this bombshell could have exploded.

'Josephine and Charlie go out to work and we all go to boring school and Mum makes sandwiches, I suppose, and we watch telly in the evenings,' Lizzie said. 'Shrimp rushed out and is crying over Bonzo. She called Uncle Trevor a big fat pig and Mum sent her out.'

All Rowan's plans lay in ruins. Swallow! What would happen to Swallow? No-one in the Pony Club would buy him, he was too naughty. He would go to market again and go from bad to worse. Those sort always did, she remembered Charlie saying once. And Cascade . . . she glanced at Hugh, and thought he looked as if he had been crying. They sat in a glum row on the feed bins.

'I can't believe it,' Rowan said.

'We're too far away from anywhere to be

a riding school, he said,' Lizzie remembered. 'No-one will come.'

'Roma's coming, and Prissy might. That's all we got from camp. I suppose it's true. Even if Josephine and Charlie were to love teaching . . .'

Rowan couldn't bear it. She went out and down to the field gate where she had stood the night before, and remembered her feelings. Now, although the sun shone and the same ponies grazed in the same place, it was as if an enormous black cloud had blotted out the sky. The change was so sudden and unexpected, she felt numb with it. Surely, to stop it happening, Josephine and Charlie could learn to like teaching! Otty did. She had said so. She loved it.

Not long afterwards, Uncle Trevor came out and Joan Hawes came down to the yard with him and stood talking by the car. They seemed quite amicable. Then he got in and drove away. Lizzie and Hugh rushed out of the feed shed and Shrimp came tearing round from Bonzo's box and they all shouted at her, 'What's going to happen? What did you tell him?'

'Nothing immediately. Don't be silly,' Joan said in her calm way. 'You know perfectly well there's nothing to worry about for the time being.'

'The time being, but what about the time after the time being?' Shrimp sobbed out.

Joan put her arm round her. 'It will be all right, pet, don't worry. You won't lose Bonzo, I'm sure.'

'What about Cascade?' Hugh said gruffly.

Joan Hawes did not answer him, but said instead, 'Come in and I'll make some lunch. None of you have eaten. And you, Rowan – are you fit this morning, or worn out?'

Rowan muttered something, unable to explain how she felt. They all went in to the kitchen and sat round the big table where Joan put out all sorts of leftovers from camp: stale rolls which she hotted up in the oven, tired salads, a couple of quiches, half an apple pie and an unpopular trifle. Charlie and Josephine were sitting together looking fed up and tired.

'What did he say? What is going to happen?' Lizzie and Hugh wanted to know.

Charlie looked glum. 'We don't move, but I work for him, here, raising his bullocks. We turn the yards into cattle yards.'

'What, Dad's lovely stables? He built them!' Hugh said. And then, almost growling, 'He wouldn't like that. Dad wouldn't like it.'

'Dad, unfortunately, isn't here any more,' Joan said.

'And what does Josephine do?' Lizzie asked.

'Josephine can work as his secretary in town. A generous offer, he said. Well-paid and three weeks' holiday a year.'

Surely she'd rather teach riding than do that, Rowan thought! She was looking rather stunned.

'All the horses and ponies would have to go. He'd want all the grass.'

'No!' shrieked Shrimp. Rowan felt herself shrieking with her, but stayed in her seat, silent and white-faced.

Lizzie said wildly, 'Have you agreed to all this? Is that what is going to happen?'

'We discussed it. No decisions have been made. He only said it was his idea, his offer to us. We didn't accept. We said we'd think about it.' Joan cut the quiches into equal portions. 'It's largely up to Josephine and Charlie, what they want to do.'

'We don't either of us want to do it. But it does mean we can all stay here and not move,' Charlie said.

'But we were going to have a riding school – High Horse! It was all arranged,' Hugh shouted out. 'Why can't we do that?'

'It won't make enough money, not that alone,' Joan said. 'I thought it might, but it means both

Josephine and Charlie getting their teaching diplomas – I learned quite a lot at camp, things I hadn't realized. Everyone has to have qualifications these days, or you get into trouble if anything goes wrong. We're in trouble anyway – a letter came from Mrs Prebble's lawyer. She's going to sue us over Birdie.'

'You never said.' Charlie sat up abruptly. 'When did it come?'

'Yesterday. I only read it late last night.'

'They wrote it before Birdie won the cup,' Charlie pointed out. 'They can hardly say we sold them a dud!'

Mrs Hawes studied the date and her face lightened. 'Yes, you're right. The date is Friday's date. Well done, Lizzie! You've saved our bacon!'

'And we were planning to visit Matty in hospital! How can she be so piggy? It *wasn't* Birdie's fault!' Shrimp cried out.

'I still think you should visit Matty, all the same,' Joan said. 'It isn't her fault her mother is – as she is.'

'How lucky I rode Birdie!' Lizzie was hugging herself with delight. 'And I was so terrified – the trouble I would get into!'

'You were great, Lizzie. Full marks,' Charlie said.

Everyone agreed. Lizzie went pink with pride.

But it made no difference to the overall sense of doom that hung over the lunch table. It seemed that Josephine and Charlie had the chief say in what was to happen, but Joan Hawes said they should carry on as they were for the time being, and give themselves time to decide.

'We're not going to be bullied by that fat butcher. He's only after what's good for him. Not what's good for us.'

Rowan went home sadly and told her mother what had happened. She cried, and her mother said, rather desperately, 'Don't, Rowan! I'll do my very best to buy you a pony, whatever happens, if it means so much to you.'

'I only want Swallow!' Rowan bawled, like a baby.

'Oh, but they say Swallow is— '

'Swallow's what? What do they say?'

'They all think he's dangerous. Even Mrs Mildmay. Why don't you want Jones? He's a lovely pony.'

'I want Swallow!'

'Oh dear,' said her mother in her old help-less way.

The day had fallen to pieces.

The next day Mrs Prebble delivered Birdie back in her horse-box and said she would sue for her money back. Mrs Hawes said they were happy to have Birdie back but would not refund the money. 'If it goes to court we can produce several witnesses – Mrs Mildmay and Mr Patterson, for example, who will testify that the pony was ridden cross-country successfully by a far less capable rider than your own daughter.'

Mrs Prebble – so the story went (the scene had been eavesdropped upon by Hugh, behind the kitchen door) – immediately burst into tears, and Joan Hawes put her arm round her and made her sit down at the table and made her a cup of tea. 'We would like to visit Matty and cheer her up. We don't want to be enemies. I am sure we can sort this Birdie thing out without going to court. We've all got enough troubles at the moment.' Perhaps then Mrs Prebble remembered that Mrs Hawes had recently lost her husband for, according to Hugh, after she had finished blubbing she turned quite nice and very nearly apologized. She said, 'Sometimes I expect too much of Matty. I can't help it. I am too competitive.'

Hearing this story, Charlie and Josephine were stunned.

'Mother works miracles! Talk about turning the other cheek!'

'Even foul Uncle Trevor – she was quite

nice to him. I don't know how she can do it.'

Then, more practically, 'What on earth are we going to do with Birdie? She's neither ours nor theirs now.'

Josephine said, 'I suppose she just wants her off her hands. No-one to exercise her, and she'll be away a lot visiting Matty.'

Josephine was rather like her mother, Rowan thought, calm and sensible.

Charlie said, offhandedly, 'It'll sort itself out. The kids can ride her.' He had been gloomy since Uncle Trevor's visit and spent most of his time working on broken-down combiners for which he was much in demand or, in the evenings, going for long rides on Wilfred across the downs, alone. Jerry Patterson offered him a job in his racing yard. He didn't know what to do. Nor did Josephine. Uncle Trevor called again – 'Just a social call. I was passing,' he said, but his eyes kept roving round the barns and stables, and out over the fields. 'You can see he's really itchy for them,' Hugh said.

It somehow made them all the more determined to thwart him.

'I couldn't work for him,' Charlie said. 'Even if he takes the yards and land. I won't be his stockman.'

'Well, that's one decision taken,' Josephine said. 'Nor could I. But what do we do? Jerry's job won't pay. Jerry's got no money himself.'

'No.'

Joan Hawes was serious about visiting Matty, whilst not pressing her two eldest in any way to come to any decisions. 'There's plenty of time.' She was going ahead with her cooking idea, and Rowan's mother went up for consultations. They reckoned they could go ahead with that, whatever happened to the farm.

Lizzie and Rowan succumbed to the hospital visit. Two was enough, Joan decided, and Hugh would be bound to say all the wrong things. They drove to the hospital on a fine August afternoon past fields of harvested corn and water meadows where the cows stood dozing in the shade of willows and alder, swishing their tails rhythmically at the flies. Lizzie and Rowan went into a decline, thinking of losing the long days pottering around with the ponies. Roma's Honeypot had arrived for 'schooling' and Roma came to ride, and Otty came over sometimes on her young horse Hadrian to school in the manège, and various small children came up for lessons but, as was painfully obvious, not enough. 'And this is the summer,' Josephine said. 'It's dark after school in the winter and no-one

146

will come.' But it was blissful just riding whatever pony was convenient, through the woods on to the downs; agonizing the knowledge that it was coming to an end. Where would the ponies go? No new homes would ever be as good as their lives at High Hawes. The depression hung like a black cloud.

Perhaps Joan Hawes thought seeing Matty would make them realize that things could be far worse. It did rather. Rowan had never been in hospital and hadn't even visited, and Lizzie's knowledge was almost as sketchy. The atmosphere was welcoming and cheerful but the sight of people in bed strung up by the legs to various contraptions was awesome, and Rowan kept her eyes glued to the floor, following Joan Hawes' feet, feeling her heart thudding with apprehension. She was aware of the health of her own legs and back; she had never thought about it before. A sideways glance at Lizzie showed her that Lizzie was feeling much the same. She looked like she did when she had decided to ride Birdie in the cross-country.

'Have you two gone dumb?' Joan said suddenly.

They looked up numbly and saw that they had arrived at a bed with Matty in it. She wasn't strung up at all, although she was lying down.

She was reading a magazine. On the cover it said 'Is your Sex Life Satisfactory?' She looked dumbstruck when she saw who her visitors were. Her white face blushed.

'Oh,' she said. Then, 'Mum didn't say— '

Neither Rowan nor Lizzie could think of a word to utter. Matty had always been Enemy Number One, but this fresh view of her rather turned the conception upside down. Joan Hawes managed to yak away without embarrassment until the two girls recovered their tongues and Matty's initial horror subsided. Then she said she was going to look for a cup of tea and departed. The three girls stared into space. Then Matty said, 'Why have you come?'

'It was Mum's idea,' Lizzie said. Then, realizing how that sounded, she added politely, 'But we had thought of it too. We thought— ' Words failed.

'When are you coming out?' Rowan asked.

'Quite soon. I'm not really bad, not going to be in a wheelchair or anything dreadful. Just it'll take a long time and my right leg doesn't work properly. It won't for ages, apparently.'

'Won't you be able to ride?'

'Well, not jump. Sit on, yes.'

'Your mum's sent Birdie back,' Lizzie said.

'You could swap her for something – quiet, perhaps.'

'Swallow?' Matty actually smiled.

'No. But Charlie could find you one.'

'I heard he went round on Out of the West?'

After the camp news was broached, conversation rattled ahead. Matty had a very jaundiced idea of what had gone on, no doubt relayed with much prejudice by her mother, and she was obviously pleased to get an unvarnished account, including one of Lizzie's ride on Birdie with Mrs Mildmay not even noticing. By the time Joan Hawes came back the three of them were shouting and laughing, and the nurse who accompanied her said, 'My word, you sound a lot more cheerful all of a sudden, young lady,' to Matty.

They made their farewells and Matty said, 'Do come again,' almost imploringly.

They departed and the nurse came with them down the corridor and said, 'That's really what the poor child needs – someone for a laugh, not that awful mother of hers forever asking how long it will be before she can compete again.'

'Does she really? Poor Matty.'

Going home in the car Lizzie and Rowan were subdued, thinking of Matty and her lot, and of how they had always hated her, and now, away from her mother, she had seemed positively nice. She hadn't bragged or sulked or said anything uppity like she usually did. Nor made any snide remarks, nor anything bad about Birdie. Lizzie said, 'I think she's enjoying having a rest, away from show-jumping.'

Joan Hawes laughed. 'Funny, I'm always trying to get you lot to do something useful instead of riding those ponies and you can't be prised away from them. And Matty, being forced all the time, doesn't really want to do it. What perverse little beasts you are!'

But afterwards, Rowan couldn't get Matty's white face and bright eyes out of her mind. She might think she had troubles herself, but they were not much compared with Matty's lot, her injury and her mother. There was no magic cure for Matty. Somehow, she thought there must be one for the High Hawes dilemma, but nobody seemed to be able to think what it was.

CHAPTER EIGHT

It was raining; soft, summer rain making the fields smell of earth and, depressingly, of winter ahead. The leaves were already beginning to turn brown and the swallows' babies were hatched out and as large as their parents. Rowan had been to two Pony Club rallies with Lizzie, Hugh and Shrimp, and ridden Fable, because Roma had bagged Jones (her father *paid*). Lizzie had ridden Birdie and Hugh Cascade, and Swallow had been left at home. Hugh said he was unreliable, and it was clear he did not want to be left out of the ribbons again. Even on Fable, Rowan had loved the rallies. Auntie Millie kept saying things like, 'Next year, at the rate you're progressing, we might get you in the Prince Philip team.' Rowan supposed gloomily she might borrow Honeypot off Roma, after she had taken over Jones. Honeypot was thinner now and rapidly becoming more active. 'He's not a bad little pony,' Charlie said, and got on him and jumped two cavallettis, lifting his feet so as not to kick them over. Rowan's inside voice wailed, 'I don't want Honeypot! I want Swallow!'

They were now back at school. Although Joan Hawes never badgered Josephine or Charlie, it was clear that decision time was due. Uncle Trevor had taken to dropping in once or twice a week – 'Just passing – dying for a cup of tea' – and every time he came he stood in the yard looking at the building with narrowed eyes, and leant on the gate looking down over the pastures towards the village. Now school had started, hardly any children came for lessons. Anyone who came had to be driven by a parent who had to wait during the lesson – 'Nobody's got that sort of time any more,' Joan pointed out. All their high hopes lay in ruins.

'Everything's horrible now,' Shrimp said. 'Charlie's so bad-tempered all the time.'

'And we hardly went to any shows at all,' Hugh said. 'Charlie wouldn't take us. Dad used to take us all the summer.'

'Only because he took the big lorry, and Josephine and Charlie showed the horses that were for sale. He didn't do it for us – we just went along because there was room in the lorry,' Lizzie pointed out.

'He liked it when we won.'

'He liked it better when Charlie or Josephine won.'

'He used to sing all the way home. And buy us ice-creams.'

They were very quiet after that. Rowan could feel the gloom palpably descending. They were riding home, the four of them, from an after-school canter across the top of the downs. The evenings were drawing in and soon, all too soon, there would be no riding after school. The valley basked in the evening sun below. They could see the horses grazing in the cool by the stream at the bottom of their fields, Swallow and Wilfred and the Armchair, and, nearer the gate, ever hopeful for a feed, Honeypot and Bonzo. Looking down on the scene, Rowan pictured it as Uncle Trevor's, the horses departed and a herd of Aberdeen Angus taking their place. She knew the others were thinking that too. She was relieved when they passed into the wood, and the great oaks shut out the view. The ponies' hooves made no sound on the soft peaty ride and none of them spoke any more.

As they came out on to the lane beside the entrance to the yard, a large car came over the hill behind them and swept past very close. Hugh yelled, 'Hogface!' and waved his fist in the air. The car slammed on its brakes and started backing up towards them. Hugh rode rapidly into the yard and the others followed, half-alarmed, half-giggling.

'He can't come in here,' Hugh shouted. 'I'll tell him he's trespassing.'

The car reversed past and came into the yard, and a large burly man got out. Hugh went rather pale but rode boldly towards him.

'You— '

'Charlie Hawes live here?' the man demanded. 'I want a word.'

Hugh gawped. The man looked familiar. Hugh noticed the number-plate on the car, HIX 1, and realized who it was.

'Mr Hicks?'

Priscilla was getting out of the passenger seat. She gave him a cool look. 'Is Charlie around?'

Hugh got off Cascade and tried to pull his wits together. This surely wasn't a social call? Was Charlie in trouble with Mr Hicks? The man never smiled; it was hard to tell. He was a hard and astute business man, said to be mega-rich.

'He's probably in the house. I'll fetch him, if you like.'

'You do that.'

The way he talked, one ran. Hugh chucked Cascade's reins at Lizzie and scuttled towards the gate. Left with the ponies, the three girls weren't sure what to do next. It seemed rather rude to walk through to the back yard and leave Mr Hicks and Prissy standing there.

'Would you like to come through?' Lizzie said. A sort of invitation.

The Hickses followed them and looked around the back yard and at the manège and down the fields. Just like Uncle Trevor. He surely didn't want to buy the place? Lizzie and Rowan both got the same thought at once.

'Oh, lor', what's he after?' Lizzie snuffled, tugging at her girth. 'Of all people—!'

'Perhaps it's Prissy – wants lessons – because she loves Charlie,' Rowan murmured.

As they turned the ponies out into the field Hugh came back with a startled-looking Charlie.

'Can I help you?'

'Yes, you can,' boomed Mr Hicks. 'Don't know how you're fixed workwise, but I've a job I'd like you to take on. That horse of ours, Out of the West – we've had top trainers in to help Priscilla but they all say the same thing – great horse but not for a girl. A lot of work to be done. You want it?'

Charlie looked stunned. The others all stood round gawping, too fascinated to politely move.

'Want it? How? What are the conditions?'

'I own it, keep it here at livery. You ride it in events, train it up to advanced level, make it worth a bomb. I'm told it's a potential star. As well as that, you find a suitable horse for Priscilla, and train it here. She can come over for lessons and compete when she's ready. Just about a full-time job, if you're free to take it on. You have the facilities. And, I'm told, the skill.'

There was a long, long silence. Rowan looked at Charlie and saw him standing like a startled deer, staring. His navy-blue gypsy eyes looked huge, wild. He didn't say anything.

Priscilla was looking at him, grinning. She wore a cream sort of tunic and tight brown trousers and her chestnut hair floated in a great cloud around her head. Was it her idea? Was it a magical offer or a minefield?

Charlie then recovered his composure and said, 'We would need to discuss it.'

'We can discuss it now.'

'Perhaps you'd better come up to the house,' Charlie said.

'Certainly.'

They departed.

Lizzie, Hugh, Shrimp and Rowan stood staring after them, their mouths hanging open.

Then Lizzie said, quite simply, 'We're saved.'

'What, by him?' Hugh said, uncertain.

'Two eventers at livery, to be trained, and lessons for Priscilla – that is *very* expensive. Charlie will make his name on Out of the West, and Mr Hicks will pay all the bills. That is how it works.'

'Then he'll sell Out of the West for a hundred thousand pounds to a foreigner.'

'Yes. But by then High Horse will be on the map.'

'Do you think—?' Rowan wondered if Charlie would seize this offer with the alacrity Lizzie seemed to assume. He did not like Mr Hicks. Charlie was very independent, and hated to be told what to do. But he adored Out of the West, and was soft on Prissy. Life was a compromise, after all. She felt a flicker of hope, and saw that the others had sort of come alight, but were afraid to put anything into words. Their cheeks were flushed, and Hugh's lower lip trembled in an odd way. He turned away, almost crossly.

'We haven't got to stay out here, just because of him. I'm starving. Mum will have tea ready.'

'I must go home,' Rowan said, routinely. But she couldn't bear to go. She didn't stay to tea after riding, not on school days.

Lizzie, understanding, said, 'I'll ring you up when he's gone, and tell you what happens.'

'Yes. You must!'

It was as if life was on hold, suddenly. A whole new picture had opened out before them, but it was hard to believe in it. Rowan realized suddenly how depressed they had all become lately. Every time they went riding they could only think of how it was going to stop soon, and the more they enjoyed themselves the worse the misery. It had become an accepted ache.

She cycled home in a dream.

Her mother had made tomato soup and a salad using up some prawns that they had decided were a bit dicey for the sandwich trade. Rowan was used to eating up leftovers, or trying out new mixes. Mr Hicks or no Mr Hicks, the Hawes and Watkins cooking partnership was making slow but steady headway. The only trouble was that the sandwich eaters, like the children who wanted to learn to ride, lived too far away. Pauline Watkins did the delivering but the cost of the petrol ate into the profits.

'We want a big factory or something, where we can sell a lot in one place.' Pauline Watkins was always alert for opportunities, and went out looking. Rowan had noticed that her mother got steadily more cheerful, just as she had got steadily more uncheerful.

She told her what had happened.

'My word! Mr Hicks is a big cheese, I

gathered. Although nobody likes him much. Poor Charlie!'

'Well, not if he gets such a good horse to ride.'

Rowan was on pins, waiting for Lizzie to ring up. She pictured Joan Hawes being calm and polite to Mr Hicks, just as she was to Uncle Trevor. They were not unalike, Mr Hicks and Uncle Trevor, wanting to take people over and tell them what to do. But Rowan didn't think anyone could tell Charlie what to do.

She helped wash up and then tried to settle down to her homework, but couldn't. When at last the phone rang, she leapt up to grab the receiver.

'Yes, Charlie's going to do it,' Lizzie said breathlessly. 'It's all right! They're going to bring the horse over, and there's going to be a sort of probationary period to see how it goes. Charlie's going to be terribly tactful. He's over the moon about getting that horse – beyond his wildest dreams he says. He was trying to make Mr Hicks see that it takes quite a long time, especially as Charlie thinks everyone has tried to make Out of the West do too much too soon. He's only five after all, and Mr Hicks thinks he ought to go round Badminton next year! Charlie explained all this and Mr Hicks took it quite well. He actually listened! Charlie called him 'sir' and Mum gave him a brandy and ginger and he was quite nice in the end. He laughed! Apparently he'd had a long talk with Auntie Millie and this was all her idea. All the people he spoke to told him Auntie Millie knew everything, and he got to believe it, he said. He almost admitted he didn't know much, which we think is a very good sign. And Charlie's got to buy another horse, for Prissy — that's two at livery! Now he's gone we're all dancing about and celebrating. Can you hear us?'

Rowan could.

'Mum's going to ring Uncle Trevor and tell him what's happened. She keeps telling us we mustn't count our chickens before they're hatched, and Charlie could easily fall out with Mr Hicks and then where will we be? But we say we won't let him. He's got to keep saying 'sir' and bowing and scraping.'

'What happens if he has a row with Prissy?' Lovers always did, after all.

'Well, apparently the Out of the West deal is nothing to do with Prissy. And we've all thought that out — if they have a tiff, Josephine can take over Prissy. She might anyway. She'd be better than Charlie.'

'Perhaps Wilfred would suit Prissy?'

'Yes, he might. But Charlie's got instructions to go out and buy something suitable. Money no object. What a lovely job!'

'And the ponies will stay!'

'Oh yes. Everything will be the same, only better!'

Rowan hadn't realized just how bad she had felt about the whole thing, until suddenly the awful threat was lifted. She felt like a new person, floating on air. When she met the others at the school bus stop in the morning, they were all bouncing again, like old times.

'Out of the West is coming tonight. You must come and see him. Charlie and Josephine are making the yard look beautiful and scrubbing out his box and turning out the tack room and mending the gate and all those things. And Ma has started singing again. You know, when she's cooking. She's a new person.'

Rowan came home, changed, and flew up to High Hawes without waiting for her tea. It was a fine evening, the air sharp with autumn and the promise of frost, and a faint mist like gauze gathering across the stream in the valley. Rowan looked at her favourite view with a feeling that it was never going to rain any more; the clouds had rolled away and God was smiling on High Hawes. Their luck had turned.

The front yard had never looked so smart. Charlie had knocked out a partition and made two boxes into one really big one, and it was filled with deep straw and a huge net of best hay hung ready. Charlie wore clean jodhpurs and a white shirt and had had a haircut, and kept saying, 'Yes, sir. That's right, sir,' so that they all got the giggles. In the event, just as it was going dusk, the enormous horse-box arrived driven by the Hicks' groom, without Mr Hicks at all, so that Charlie's efforts to look God-fearing and clean were wasted.

The groom, an older man, climbed down from the cab and came round to open up the cab.

'Can't say as I'll be sorry to lose this one,' he said. 'Too much energy for 'is own good. Nothing but trouble.'

'Too strong for Miss Hicks,' Charlie said politely.

The man grunted contemptuously. 'Should go back to racing, what 'e was bred for. The Grand National should suit 'im nicely.'

Charlie looked in no way abashed by this information. Rowan knew that he thought most horses were underworked and overfed. Out of the West hadn't been turned out since he had been bought by the Hicks.

They dropped the ramp and the groom led

out the gorgeous horse. He stood looking all round him with his large, intelligent eyes, then let out a challenging whinny. Wilfred, already installed as his neighbour, answered with his sweet, high-pitched nicker and danced about behind his door. They led Out of the West into his new box and let him loose and he walked all round sniffing and pawing at the straw and generally making a great mess of the carefully arranged bedding, then came to the door and let out some more bellows. From way down the field behind the yard the ponies answered him. Charlie laughed. Then he took the groom into the tack room and they discussed feeding and the horse's foibles. Joan Hawes offered the man a drink in the house, but he said he had better be getting back, so the impressive horse-box departed and left the younger Hawes and Rowan capering round the yard with excitement, until Charlie told them to clear off and leave his horse to settle.

Rowan stayed to tea and afterwards went to see Swallow in the field. His winter coat was starting to grow, with its blue-black lustre deepening across the flanks, with faint dapples stippling his belly, and his muzzle softening to gingery brown. Out of the West was much the same colour – perhaps even the same character?

– Rowan was struck by the comparison. Swallow was sweet and affectionate in the field and stable, and wouldn't hurt a fly. Why did he have to be such a difficult ride? Perhaps, as Charlie maintained, if he was ridden and worked hard every day, he would settle and become more amenable. But even in the holidays he did not get that much work. And in schooltime – there just wasn't that much time in the day. Rowan stroked his velvety muzzle.

'I *will* ride you,' she vowed. 'I will get good enough.'

It was amazing to think that she had even got this far in only seven months. A year ago she hadn't even set eyes on Swallow. She found it hard to think back to her life in Putney before they moved to the country, and to the days before she had discovered ponies, and the Hawes.

Out of the West was not an easy horse. Charlie decided to let him down and work him over the downs on long hacks, and not jump him nor do dressage training until he had settled into his new home and got over some of his hang-ups. He had told Mr Hicks not to expect quick results. It was one of his conditions. Mr Hicks, advised by Auntie Millie, had agreed.

After a week, Out of the West was turned out into the home field. He careered round madly, while Charlie stood anxiously watching, but eventually he settled and started to graze. The ponies had all come up to the fence from the bottom field and stood in a row staring at him. The big horse moved about restlessly, switching his tail. Charlie leaned over the fence, chewing a piece of grass.

'As long as he doesn't jump out, we're OK.'

Rowan didn't know this was something horses did.

'Big horse like him – the fence across the end, against the down, isn't really high enough. All right for the ponies, but we've had a colt jump out once, when some people went by on horses that way.'

Charlie had never had to handle horses that didn't belong to him, and found the valuable horse a worry he hadn't foreseen. Standards at High Hawes were somewhat slapdash, and the whole regime would have to be tightened now he was virtually a professional.

'The ponies need clipping. They look like wild things. You can fetch them in and get the mud off them for a start, and get their boxes cleaned out and ready.'

The days were shortening and the leaves were blowing about the fields. Charlie and Josephine spent a lot of time out looking for the right young horse for Priscilla. 'The sooner we get it in the yard, the sooner our income increases.' Meanwhile she came once a week for lessons with Josephine on Wilfred, but she didn't like Wilfred. He didn't go for her, because she was a weak rider and exerted no authority, so he dropped back into his lazy riding-school habits. Both Charlie and Josephine realized quickly that to get a suitable horse for Prissy to compete on – and hopefully win, to keep her father sweet – was going to be difficult. A push-button jumper, which did not hot up . . . which could win in big company with a passenger rider.

'They're rare.' Charlie discussed it at length with his sister. 'Like gold dust. I think we shall have to persevere with Wilfred. We know he's safe, and willing enough if she gets her act together.'

'I reckon she might well get on with Birdie,' Josephine said.

'More than our life's worth. Officially Birdie still belongs to Mrs Prebble.'

'We'd better start sending her bills for keep then.'

'I think Rowan could ride Birdie, given time, if she'd drop her fixation for Swallow.'

'She wants her mother to buy Swallow.'

'That would be unwise. He has a very dubious

past – on the loose and lost for several weeks, then stolen, sold on the market – who knows that his real owners might not turn up one day, especially if we take him to shows or events? Somewhere along the line he was very well-schooled and taught to jump. It's really weird nobody ever enquired after him.'

'All I can say, he must have had a pretty good rider.'

'Yes. He's for Hugh, if he's for anybody. He's a boy's pony.'

Rowan did not hear this conversation, busy carrying out orders, carting new straw into the ponies' boxes. The ponies were to be trace clipped, and their rugs sorted out from the tack room.

The next Saturday Rowan went to High Hawes to find that Joan Hawes had decided to take Lizzie, Hugh and Shrimp – much against their will – shopping for winter school things. 'Everyone else does it in August,' she snapped at them, as they grizzled. She didn't like shopping either. Charlie and Josephine had gone to look at a horse in Devon. Charlie had ridden Out of the West earlier, and he was now turned out, with instructions to be brought in when the shoppers came home. All the ponies had been clipped except Swallow, who was shut in his box to keep clean until Charlie returned, when he said he would do him. The others were out down the bottom of the field in their freshly scrubbed New Zealand rugs.

'So you're in charge, Rowan,' Joan Hawes said as she backed her ancient car out of its shed. 'We won't be away for long – you can all ride after lunch.'

'I'll groom Swallow, and sweep the yard.'

'Otty might come over to school Hadrian.'

'OK.'

They departed. Rowan went and leaned on the fence and watched Out of the West for a bit, who looked fantastic, unclipped and with a coat gleaming with wellbeing. It was very easy to waste time just looking at horses. Out of the West, with his beautiful but not handy name, had been rechristened Jack, and was grazing peacefully with Wilfred. All the ponies except Swallow were in their favourite spot at the bottom of the field, too far away to talk to, so Rowan fetched a box of grooming tools and set to work on Swallow. Charlie had taught her how to groom, throwing her weight behind the brush – 'Not just a tickle. It should be really hard work,' so Rowan conscientiously did the job properly and had the satisfaction of seeing the dark coat coming up from under the layer of dried mud with its accustomed shine. Funny how she didn't mind this sort of hard work . . .

Strangely, in the distance she could hear voices. She looked out of the stable and saw a couple of riders coming up the hill from the village on the far side of the top field. Quite a strong wind was blowing, and one of the riders was having trouble with his horse which was bucking and trying to take off. They were shouting and laughing, and Rowan heard one of them yell, 'Oh, come on! Let them go – they want to!' They were far away but Rowan could sense the fun and excitement and found herself smiling. But Out of the West sensed it too, and started to trot along the fence beside them. The riders went on, taking no notice. Out of the West reared up, the wind in his tail – he looked magnificent – spun round and galloped back the other way, down towards the ponies, then he reared up again, flung himself round and, in one almighty jump, cleared the fence out of the field.

Rowan, watching and laughing, felt her jaw drop in horror. What had been a bit of fun was now major disaster. The horse was galloping away up the hill, bucking as he went with pure spirits, excited by the horses far in front of him.

Whether their riders would see him and try to catch him Rowan had no way of knowing, for very shortly the edge of the wood above the house cut them off from her view, and Out of the West as well.

She dropped her grooming tools and stood fastened to the ground like a zombie. She was completely alone, and the whole future of High Hawes was on the loose out on the downs. Out of the West could go for miles, come to a road and get hit by a car, he could fall down the chalk quarry, break a leg, or get completely lost and distressed, not to be found for days . . . her imagination pictured the worst.

Before he got too far away, she ought to make an effort to keep up with him, see where he went. What would Charlie do? He would get out the Land-Rover and drive after him over the downs. She couldn't do that. Her bike would be hopeless up there. The answer was to ride after him, take a head-collar and try to catch him. With a pony, he might even follow her back.

She looked out of the door. All the ponies were miles away, and had their winter rugs on. By the time she got one out of the field, which was always a tangle for her, opening the gate and shoving the others out of the way, and stripped and saddled and bridled it, Out of the West would be miles away. The answer, of course, was standing right beside her, breathing down her neck – Swallow. His saddle and bridle were in the tack room next door and he was groomed and polished and ready to go.

Rowan ought to have hesitated, but strangely her heart leapt up at the challenge – she had no alternative! Nobody could blame her for taking Swallow.

'You *will* behave, won't you? You *will*, Swallow!'

Was it an appeal or a command? She didn't know, sliding the saddle hastily on to his back and grabbing for the girth. She remembered to run for a big head-collar, and stuff her pocket with horse nuts which always helped with catching. In two minutes she was leading Swallow out and scrambling into the saddle. The stirrup leathers were right, thank goodness – she kicked him heartily in the ribs and he was out in the lane making for the path through the woods at a surprised trot. Normally, like good children, they always walked for the first ten minutes. Now, once on the path under the trees, Rowan asked him to canter.

Swallow liked this. He set off with a preliminary buck to show what a good mood he was in, but Rowan sat this without any trouble.

Her blood was up and she almost wanted him to buck again, and again, because she *knew* she wouldn't come off. She had never felt this confident before. It mattered so terribly – dear Charlie's whole life depended on it! She could hardly believe what was happening, the suddenness of it!

Out of the woods and on to the downs she asked Swallow to gallop up the long grassy hill. There was no sign of Out of the West below, nor of the two riders, but she thought once she breasted the top of the hill and could see in all directions, she was bound to see them. With luck the two riders would help her – they might already have had the sense to catch the loose horse. Swallow loved going fast and when he slowed for a breather she kicked him on again, and he responded like a little race horse, although beginning to blow. Rowan was beginning to blow too. She had never ridden so fast so far before. The hill got steep near the top but they scrambled up, and the wind met them, whistling up from the other side. Swallow put in another buck, this one more unexpected, and Rowan lost a stirrup.

'Pig!' The first fine rapture of the chase was now starting to wear off a bit, and anxiety was taking its place. What if she couldn't even find out where the horse had gone? The downs were huge once one was on the top, rolling north, east and west like the backs of great basking pigs, hazed in the distance with the soft mist of autumn which almost hid the maze of lanes and villages beyond. Out of the West could eat up miles with his long stride.

She looked back down the home valley and there was no sign of anything moving. She continued up on to the ridge and looked down the other side towards the site of the Pony Club camp. Nothing. The world was totally deserted. She almost wondered if she had been dreaming, that Out of the West was still happily grazing in his field. But, looking down, she could see that he wasn't, unless he was in the corner hidden by the wood, which was unlikely. She had to ride on and see over the ridge to the east, then she would have covered all directions. He must be there.

She put Swallow into a trot. He seemed to have sensed her seriousness for he did not play up again. Perhaps the gallop had taken the tickle out of him. As she rode she wondered how on earth she was going to catch the big horse – she had never even led him before, feeling scared of his size and her puny strength should he disagree with her. Now she was planning to lead him tamely home on a leading-rein like a pet dog. But find him first.

The ground flattened out ahead of her and then started to run downhill, and at last she could see the whole of the landscape to the east. She pulled Swallow up and frowned into the distance. A chalky lane wound up from the valley between high banks of trees, and she could see the two riders disappearing down it, but Out of the West was not with them and it was apparent that they were not aware of him, for they seemed relaxed. Something moving caught her eye to the right, half hidden by a rise in the ground. Swallow swung his head round suddenly and stood staring towards the spot, his ears pricked tight. Then he gave a whinny.

Rowan waited, very tense. Then a familiar head appeared over the rise in the ground and Out of the West trotted out into view about a quarter of a mile below her, coming in her direction. Swallow saw him and gave another whinny, piercing this time and plunged forward so suddenly that this time Rowan nearly fell off. She just managed to grab a handful of mane and haul herself to safety, then had to gather up the snatched reins to pull him up. Out of the West was coming towards them now at a canter, kicking up his heels every now and then with excitement, just like Swallow.

Rowan had no idea what to do. She wasn't sure she had control over Swallow, and now the idea of catching Out of the West and leading him tamely home seemed preposterous.

So she stood there and felt Swallow dancing beneath her as the big horse approached. In her nervousness she tightened the reins and as Swallow snatched at his bit she knew she was doing exactly what Josephine always warned against, tensing up and making Swallow cantankerous. But how could she relax? She was frightened.

Out of the West came up, snorting and tossing his head. Rowan could see that he was very excited, his nostrils flared wide and red. He came so close she felt the heat of his breath, then he spun round and let out the most enormous bucking kick. His shod hooves whistled past her leg and landed on Swallow's flank with a jolt that Rowan felt beneath her. Swallow gave an angry squeal, snatched himself round and let fly in return, which Rowan felt as a large buck. She shot up Swallow's neck, landing round his ears, and all but came off, but pure fear and a healthy sense of self-preservation compelled her into doing the right thing, shoving herself back in the saddle, turning Swallow quickly round to face Out of the West and driving him on to ride past, heading for home. She had to exert command.

Swallow nervously went on and Out of the West, to Rowan's surprised relief, followed. But there was no indication that he was going to stay for long, for he was looking all around him, stopping and starting, and seemed likely to lose interest in Swallow quite shortly. The thought of him plunging off over the top of the downs after she had actually found him was chastening. Charlie would never forgive her if she let him get away now.

But catching him was a two-handed job. Could she manage it without letting go of Swallow? Handling one pony was all she had been asked to do up to now: the job before her was horrific. Unless the horse lowered his head she could not even reach high enough to get the head-collar on.

But she had no choice.

She got off Swallow. Her hands trembled as she shook out the head-collar and got it the right way up. Out of the West wandered off while she was doing this and started grazing. At least his head was in the right place now. If only there was something to tie Swallow up to! But there was nothing for miles. She knew she couldn't let him go, because if he decided to kick up his heels and gallop off and Out of the West went with him she would be in worse trouble than ever. So she pulled his reins over his head and looped them over her arm, and approached the big horse warily. From the front, as Charlie had taught her. Swallow tried to graze too, but she pulled him up with a yank.

She had a pocketful of nuts, she remembered. As she got close, and Out of the West made no move to go, she threw some of the nuts down in front of his nose. Forgetting Swallow – that was a mistake – for he greedily dived forward . . . Out of the West tossed up his head, turned and trotted off for several paces. He stood, looking round. Rowan was almost weeping with tension.

'Come on, Jack – look what I've got!' she wheedled, holding out her hand with the nuts in.

Swallow barged in and gobbled them up before she had a chance to shove him off.

'You beast!'

But Out of the West saw that she had something of interest and took a step forward.

Risking everything, Rowan scattered the rest of the nuts on the ground and let go of Swallow. As Out of the West's head went down she managed to hold out the noseband of the head-collar in just the right place, getting it under his chin before his lips touched the grass. To her everlasting relief, he let her halter him without a fuss, and she got the buckle done up safely. He went forward with his ears back, warning Swallow off the titbits. Rowan made a sideways dive to grab Swallow's reins, but couldn't reach them. Swallow turned round and walked away, the reins trailing on the ground.

Now she had Out of the West, but Swallow was loose, saddled and bridled.

Rowan didn't know whether to laugh or cry.

She had no more nuts left to tempt Swallow with. Out of the West seemed disposed to go on grazing. If only someone would come! But in her experience, they hardly ever met anyone up here. She knew perfectly well that Jones would have been easy to catch, so would Cascade and even Birdie, but Swallow was often difficult, unless one carried titbits.

At least she had the valuable one. She was very nervous of his size, and getting her feet trodden on, but when she walked forward he came with her quite happily. She decided to take him home first, and hope Swallow would tag along. She hadn't even run his stirrups up, and the trailing reins invited disaster, but there was nothing she could do about it now.

She walked firmly on. In spite of Swallow being loose, she felt shakily triumphant at having caught Out of the West. She felt rather tearful, and it seemed an awful long way back to High Hawes, the way she had come so fast on Swallow.

Swallow seemed disposed to come with them, but every time she went towards him to try and catch him he trotted away, treading on his reins and pulling himself up short, then trotting on. Rowan decided to leave him. She didn't want him to excite Out of the West, for if he decided to pull away from her she knew she would never hold him.

How wonderful if the family were to come back early and come sweeping up the hill towards her on their ponies! But nothing happened and it was a long, anxious walk. Out of the West came tamely for the most part, but sometimes he would stop and pull back, and gaze out over the valley as if in two minds to gallop off, but each time she spoke to him softly and urged him on and, all in his own good time, he came. Swallow, stopping mostly to graze, dropped away behind, and eventually became lost to view.

When she got back she put Out of the West

in his box, and burst into tears. She couldn't stop trembling and crying, and kept thinking how stupid she was. She knew she had to go back and find Swallow, and she guessed he would be harder to catch than Out of the West. This time she took several handfuls of nuts in a bucket and trudged back through the wood on to the down. But there was no sign of Swallow anywhere, and it was a long way to the top without a pony. She decided the best thing would be to saddle up Jones and go searching, so she turned and started trudging back. But as she did so she saw Charlie's Land-Rover coming back up the hill and swing into the yard, and all her troubles fell away. She ran.

From the wood she could hear the telephone bell ringing in the yard (it was wired to be heard in the manège, although the telephone was in the tack room). She thought nothing of it until, turning in through the gateway, she saw Charlie come running out of the tack room and jump into the Land-Rover again.

He turned it round furiously and shouted at her out of the window, 'Who told you to go out on Swallow? There's been an accident on the road and they say it's one of our ponies!'

His eyes blazed. Without waiting for her, he shot out of the yard and roared away up the hill.

CHAPTER NINE

This time Rowan really cried. She howled.
Poor Swallow was killed and it was all her
fault, and no-one would ever believe what had
happened.

She had forgotten all about Josephine who
suddenly came out of the tack room to see what
the noise was.

'Whatever—?'

'It's not fair!' Rowan heard herself crying out,
like a baby. 'I – I didn't— '

'Rowan! Shut up!'

'I couldn't help it! I did – did – what I
thought – was best – and Charlie – Charlie
shouted at me!'

'Oh, Rowan, calm down and tell me what
happened.'

The voice was calm and sympathetic, not cross
like Charlie's, and Rowan managed to control
her sobs, although she felt shaken to the core.

'I only rode out on Swallow because Out

of the West jumped out of his field and galloped away. I caught him, but then Swallow ran off— '

'Rowan!'

Josephine looked thunderstruck. Through her tears Rowan saw the shock on her face. She came up close and put her arms round Rowan and hugged her.

'Stop crying! You're a heroine! We wondered why Jack was back in his box and the others not home – and he'd been sweating. We were just talking about it, and then the phone rang— '

'What did they say about Swallow? He's not hurt, is he?'

Another great outpouring of tears at the thought of darling Swallow lying mangled in the road . . . the first time she had set eyes on Swallow was when her father hit him with his car on the road – it seemed years ago now. And it was all her fault, because she had been too stupid to catch him.

'I don't know. They didn't say the pony was hurt, only that a car was in a ditch. He'll probably be OK, if the car swerved. Don't worry! Ponies have a great sense of self-preservation, not like thoroughbreds. Tell me what happened— '

Rowan, calming down, told Josephine the

story of chasing Out of the West. Josephine was full of praise and admiration.

'You did wonderfully well to catch him! That matters more than anything – whatever would we have done if we'd come home and found him missing! Letting go of Swallow was the best thing to do. You're brilliant!'

Josephine gave Rowan a real hug, and Rowan's despair gave way to an unusual flicker of self-esteem.

'Poor Rowan – all that and then Charlie bawls you out – come along, let's go and make a cup of tea.'

Rowan followed her across the garden to the house. Rowan had never made much contact with Josephine before, apart from during her riding lessons, and her warmth now surprised her. She was always rather quiet, cool and beautiful, and – Rowan had always felt – unapproachable. But she had never been alone with her before, nor in such a state. Sitting down at the familiar kitchen table, she now felt ashamed of her hysterics. She felt tired, as if it were bedtime instead of not even lunchtime. Josephine produced a strong cup of tea and a large tinful of chocolate biscuits.

'Don't worry about Swallow. On the phone it was all about the car, and the driver who was in a rage. They never said anything about injuries.'

'Oh, good. Or will you have to pay for the car?' A terrible thought now assailed her, that a large bill for damages would be forthcoming.

'We're insured for that. We're not that stupid. But losing Out of the West like that – I can't think of a worse disaster! I shouldn't think any of the others could have done better, getting him back like that.'

Hot tea and praise warmed Rowan through. She felt as if she were going to melt, exhausted by her traumas. After her unburdening of all her troubles, she remembered what Josephine and Charlie had gone out for.

'Did you buy a horse?'

'No. But we liked it.' Her eyes went dreamy. '*I* liked it. Oh, I would like it!'

'You mean for you, not for Priscilla?'

'Yes.'

It had never occurred to Rowan before that, of them all, Josephine didn't have her own horse. She was always riding, but always other people's, schooling or training – like Charlie, who had lost Fedora and bought only cheap, thin Wilfred for himself.

'Charlie thinks it will be too much for Priscilla.'

'Like Out of the West.'

'Yes. But not as unsuitable as him. I just thought – ' Her voice trailed off. Rowan waited, interested. 'I suppose it's dishonest.'

'What?'

'Buy this one for Priscilla, and it will be unsuitable for her. But Charlie and I could make it – I know we could – and perhaps – perhaps – ' She hesitated, then shrugged.

'Mr Hicks will say, you ride it? Like Out of the West?'

Josephine grinned. 'Yes. It's dishonest, isn't it?'

Rowan considered. 'A bit, I think. If you really think it isn't suitable. But then Mr Hicks could always say sell it again, and you would have improved it, and you can make him a profit.'

Josephine looked hopeful. 'Yes. That's very sensible. You're really bright, Rowan.' A long pause. 'Not very fair on Priscilla though.'

They both laughed.

At that moment the telephone rang again. Josephine answered it.

'Oh, Jerry, hullo!'

Rowan, thinking it might be Charlie about Swallow, sank back in her chair and took another chocolate biscuit. Jerry seemed to do all the talking and Josephine kept saying yes.

After some time she said, 'Yes, I'm sure we're interested. When Charlie gets in I'll tell him.'

She put the phone down and came back to the table.

'You won't believe this, but that was Jerry Patterson saying he might have a horse that would suit Priscilla.'

'Oh dear,' Rowan said.

Josephine grinned. 'Bad timing.'

'Perhaps she could have two horses. If Mr Hicks is so rich.'

'This one is a racehorse, but so laid back Jerry says it will never win a race. But very good-looking, a very easy ride and a good jumper. And cheap.'

'Probably too cheap for Mr Hicks. He likes expensive things.'

'Yes.'

'He might like the idea of Priscilla having two horses. She could start on Jerry's and improve enough to ride yours.'

Josephine laughed. 'Well, we're not short of ideas, dishonest or otherwise. We'll see.'

Rowan was on pins waiting for Charlie to come back. She couldn't be sure Swallow wasn't hurt, in spite of Josephine's encouraging words. If Swallow was all right she would feel fantastic, Josephine having told her she was a heroine, brilliant, sensible and bright. Not bad for one morning.

But it wasn't long before the rattle of the Land-Rover echoed across the garden. Rowan leapt up.

Josephine said quickly, 'I'll tell him what happened,' and went out ahead of her. Rowan trailed behind, her heart thumping with apprehension. She hung back as she watched the two of them talking, Charlie still sitting in the Land-Rover. Then, after a bit, he got out and slammed the door. He looked stunned, as Josephine had at the news of the near disaster, and went instinctively over to the horse's box and looked him over.

Rowan, judging the smoke had cleared, advanced.

'Is Swallow all right?'

Charlie swung round.

'Yes.' He looked lost for words, obviously still thinking what he might have had to be saying to Mr Hicks if Out of the West had been lost. 'I – Jeez, Rowan — ' Words failed him. He came forward and put an arm round her shoulder. 'I'm sorry I shouted. You're a marvel.'

'What happened to Swallow? Is he all right?'

'Yes.' 'What a near squeak, eh? What an idiot I was, not to think — ' He gave himself a mental shake. 'Yes, your Swallow's OK. He just ran out into the lane at the top of the hill as a car was coming down. The car swerved into the ditch and more or less crumpled up, but the driver's all right. Only a bit mad – you can say that again. Guess who it is?' A wide grin stretched across his face suddenly.

'Who?'

'Mrs Prebble.'

'No!'

They couldn't help roaring with laughter, until Josephine recovered herself and said, 'Oh, no, we mustn't laugh – poor Mrs Prebble! She can't do without a car, with Matty in hospital.'

'Matty's coming home tomorrow,' Charlie said. 'That was part of the diatribe – what's she going to do without a car to fetch Matty in? I said she could borrow ours.'

'She wouldn't be seen dead in ours!'

'Yes, she more or less told me that. Well, I did my best.' Charlie shrugged. 'At least the pony's all right. She always drives far too fast. Visibility's perfect on the hill. She should have had plenty of time to stop. We'd better go and collect him. I left him tied up in Mr Herbert's barn, till Hugh gets back.'

'I'll go,' Rowan said. '*Please*!'

Charlie looked at her and gestured to the Land-Rover. 'Hop in.'

She hopped. Charlie turned round and drove out of the yard.

'What you did today ... you know how important it was, don't you? My life, just about.'

'Yes.'

'I shall never be able to thank you enough. None of the kids could have done better.'

'They might have caught Swallow. Hugh would have.'

'Blow Hugh.'

Charlie changed gear as the Land-Rover met the brow of the hill. Then he said, 'Look, for better or for worse, think of Swallow as yours. Between us, we'll make him behave. I shall never let you ride an unsafe pony, but I don't think we'll let him beat us. He's got so many qualities. He just needs to learn a bit of sense. We can teach him sense between us, you and me and Josephine. We'll take time with him.'

Rowan wasn't sure if she'd got it right. 'Mine?'

'Yours, with provisos.' Charlie laughed. 'You know perfectly well we can't sell him – no-one'll have him. You must do as you're told. Never, never ride without supervision. Not until he's safe. Unless Out of the West jumps out of his field, of course.'

'Oh, Charlie!' She couldn't speak.

They came to Mrs Prebble's Audi lying crumpled in the ditch, with the breakdown van labouring towards it up the hill from the other side, then Charlie drove away down a farm track and pulled up in a barnyard. He stopped the engine and turned and looked at her.

'You're a great girl, Rowan,' he said.

Then he opened the door and got out.

Rowan followed him into the old barn, high and cool like a rough-hewn cathedral. Swallow stood resting a hind leg, his nose in a corner. When he saw them, he lifted his head and fluttered his nostrils. Rowan went up to him and buried her face into his forelock. She was crying again and wanted to hide it. She felt so stupid, crying all day long like a ninny, in spite of being a heroine and a great girl. It was all too much for her. But when she looked up, Charlie was taking the saddle off.

'Lead him back,' he said.

'But— '

'This time, Rowan. He's had a very disturbing morning. Running away, nearly hit by a car – it would be very stupid to have your first authorized ride on him after all that. You lead him home quietly for now.'

'Yes.'

It was true. If Swallow felt anything like she did, he would keel over before they went far. They untied him and led him out into the sunlight. Charlie put the saddle in the car. He went to get into the driving seat, and turned back.

'Another thing,' he said. 'It might not work. Remember that.'

'What do you mean?'

'For all we school him, he might always be too strong and dangerous for you. And there'll be no answer to that. You'll have to accept it. Accepting disappointment is the biggest thing of all to learn when it comes to horses. Ask anyone – Auntie Millie, Jerry, Mrs Prebble – from racing right down to ponies. Don't forget, Rowan, that I told you that.'

His gypsy dark eyes were very serious.

'No. I won't forget.'

He drove on and she started to lead Swallow down the farm track. Her head was swimming. So many things ahead of her – all sorts of things starting to happen: Josephine scheming to get the horse she had fallen in love with, Out of the West to be proved a star eventer, Priscilla

191

to be made happy, High Hawes to thrive, and Swallow . . . Swallow to learn to bend his will to hers. Charlie's warning rang in her ears.

But for now . . . the sun was shining. She was a marvel and a heroine, and Swallow was walking beside her, quiet and gentle. The downs stretched before her, disturbed only by the lane snaking down to High Hawes. Where I belong, thought Rowan. Me and Swallow. There was certainly nothing to cry about any more.

THE END